BRIGHTEN

THE CORNER

WHERE YOU ARE

Books by Fred Chappell

Fred Chappell

BRIGHTEN

THE CORNER

WHERE YOU ARE

St. Martin's Press   New York

Parts of this novel, often in quite different form, first appeared in *Arete, Epoch, New Mexico Humanities Review, Now and Then, Pembroke Magazine,* and *Quarterly West.*

DESIGN BY JUDITH A. STAGNITTO

Library of Congress Cataloging-in-Publication Data

Chappell, Fred, 1936–
    Brighten the corner where you are / Fred Chappell.
        p.   cm.
    ISBN 0-312-03297-8
    I. Title.
PS3553.H298B75   1989
813'.54—dc20   89-30426
                                                          CIP

10   9   8   7   6   5   4   3   2

For my mother

Contents

MOON

We walked along the crackling road. Those winter mornings were so cold that I felt I would ring like an anvil if my father touched me. A shining frost lay over everything, even the stones, so tough it seemed a knife could not pierce it, and the strands of barbwire were frosted so that the fence that bordered the road looked like guitar strings.

There was no moon and the constellations were caught in the top of the great walnut tree below the road like sparkling wisps of hay. As we passed beneath the trees, I watched these stars tangled in the bare black limbs; they were as unsteady and restless as fireflies.

When there was a moon, the world was all different. The trees and rocks and fence posts and spikes of dead weeds in the ditches—everything was as still as eternity and shone a pure lyric silver. The moon erased the stars; the whole sky was a granular mist of silver. The moon spread about itself like a threshing machine sending up dust in the wheat field; and the moon itself was larger and closer than the barn. My father and I bent our heads to duck below it, and once it scraped my head as I went underneath and knocked off my blue wool cap. I picked it up and brushed at the hard silver moon-mist that was colder than the frost, colder than icicles. My fingers twitched with sparkling fire.

"There is too much moon," I said.

"It is just too large," my father said. "When it gets as large as this, it is impossible to handle."

Then we came to the barn and went down the path to the milking room below road level and there was another moon waiting for us. On the little window there beside the door, in one of the four velvet panes of glass, the moon floated small and white and flat, no larger than a softball.

"All right then," my father said. "Maybe we can figure out something about it now. First we'll milk the cows and do the other chores."

So we did. We fed the horses and pigs and I milked two cows while he milked four and then we were ready to go back to the house and pour up the milk and wash and eat breakfast. As we went out the milking room door, my father stopped and turned and ripped the moon from the window and thrust it down into one of the buckets of milk and clapped a lid over it. His movement had been so swift and smooth that I did not understand at first what he had done, but when he stood licking the milk foam from his fingers and looking smug and pleased with himself, I knew what had happened and I grew afraid. "You've taken it down," I said. "You stole the moon!"

"Yes," he said. "I did. I certainly did do that. It was about time that somebody gave it a try. I've been thinking about it for ages."

Now that there was no longer any moon in the sky, there were more stars than we had ever imagined. Constellations appeared that no one had ever seen and my father had to name them for us: White Monkey, Brunel's Hat, Fan Vault, Old Hickory, Johnson's Powderpuff, The Vanishing Cathedral, Tithonus, Darwin's Destiny, Stir Crazy, and many others.

That was fun for a while, but even in the early days we felt a sense of loss and this feeling worsened as the months went on. We missed the moon and began to long for it. Yes, there were more stars now, but they were farther distant than the ones we had always known before and they shed little light; they seemed to increase the darkness, or at least to emphasize it more deeply.

We were lonesome for the moon in the sky; it was no use at all in the little room there off the kitchen where we stored the fresh milk. My father had transferred it from the galvanized milk pail to one of the big steel cans that had already been half-full of milk. He had set the big can in the corner and we hardly even glanced at it when we worked in the room.

The truth is that we didn't dare look at it. The outside of the can was rimed with the grainy moon-silver that sometimes made shapes like words we could not quite make out; perhaps these words were in a lunar language no one knew. Sometimes the steel would glow silver-white and make the room cooler by sensible degrees. On those nights when the moon used to be full and sliding over the sky like a smooth nude figurehead on the prow of a silver ship, the steel can would roll wildly across the floor and slam into the *walls. The moon was trying to surge up to its proper roost in the solar system.*

Then one day my father said, "Oh, all right, all right," and he opened the steel can to find only a cool creamy cheese that filled it to the very top. It was a lovely unmarred pure cheese, but when we tasted it, smearing it on our mouths with our fingers, we found that it had no savor at all, bland as snow and almost as cold.

"Oh, all right," my father said, "I give up."

That night at midnight, he climbed onto the roof of the barn and I steadied the can as he drew it up to him with a rope tied to the handle. The night seemed darker than at any time before in the lengthy story of the world. My grandmother and my mother had come to watch, and my sister Mitzi slept in my mother's arms. My father pried the top off the can and flung it away into the darkness. Then he plunged his hands into the moon-cheese and held them toward the sky. At first nothing happened except that the candescent substance melted in his warm hands and ran glowing down his arms and dripped on his pants and shoes and spattered twinkling on the roof about his feet. But he kept thrusting his hands into the beautiful creamy stuff and holding it aloft until finally it did begin to rise in little streams like quicksilvers rising in so many thermometers ranked side by side. Little by little the customary forces were taking hold and the cheese began to rise into the sky in steady streams as my father dipped it out of the big can. The attraction became so strong that it even lifted him a few inches off the roof, so he stepped back and let it pour heavenward in a steady stream like a column of marble.

It rose and rose into the sky so far that we could not trace its course and when it was all gone, the night was dark.

And then, after a minute or two of terrible blackness, the moon was there again, full at the top of the sky, and everything was back to the way it had been before. The night *birds sang and the insects and we breathed more easily and freely and looked about us at the world the moon made visible.*

When my father came down the ladder, clumsily struggling with the empty steel can, my grandmother was waiting. In the good new moonlight, we could see that she was mostly happy and relieved but also curious and vexed. "What made you take it down in the first place, Joe Robert?" she asked. "Why didn't you leave it just well enough alone?"

"Hey, it was worth finding out, wasn't it?" he said. "If I didn't do it, maybe nobody ever would. Then we'd never know, would we? But now we know."

She only shook her head in sorrowful wonder. My grandmother believed that knowledge and wisdom were two separate things entirely and not even closely connected; she thought it possible that knowledge could sometimes be the bitter enemy of wisdom.

But for my father, knowledge was the necessary precondition for wisdom; he thought that he needed to acquire a great deal of knowledge to ponder on until he formed it into wisdom, the way a sculptor shapes a statue from his stone. He believed, too, that this notion marked him as the champion of modern scientific attitude. In fact, he was the local champion of reason and science, but somehow he had gotten mounted backward on his noble charger, and his shining armor clattered eerily about him like a tinware peddler's cart.

One

THE

DEVIL-POSSUM

Who can tell us what my father was doing at three o'clock in the morning of a balmy May Friday in 1946?

Why, he was climbing a medium-sized intricate poplar tree, hugging himself up the trunk and clambering among the limbs like a child dazed by dreams of pirate mizzenmasts. A muddy old totesack he clenched in his teeth, and a savor of the burlap was to remain in his mouth through all this long day to come. The four hounds leaping and yapping below had treed the fearful devil-possum and Joe Robert Kirkman was all fixed to capture the animal and take him home and put him to some private use not virtuous in the least.

This was no dignified impulse for a thirty-six-year-old country schoolteacher to act upon, a grown man with a family and serious responsibilities, but it was the sort of adventure he was always eagerly into, Satan take the world and all its prune-faced disapproval. And it was only impulse on his part, because the settled tradition among his houndy associates was never to lay eyes upon any game the dogs stirred up. The creatures in the trees and thickets and pungent dens were assigned to the dogs; the men's big task was to loll by the campfire and nurse their conversation.

Which is what they'd been doing, old Pauley Mackail and Wylie Hazel and Broomsedge Tommy Fowler, and my father familiar among them and just as easy as they, until the notion occurred that he could *do* something with that possum they could hear the dogs had treed, that he could pack it home and cause interesting events to take place in our family life. He could—well, he might pop it into the cookstove and when my grandmother went to bake her biscuits, there would be a live possum in the oven, and that would give her something to think about. He was just certain that his strict-souled mother-in-law needed something to think about.

But it went rudely against the grain of the Crazy Creek Wildlife Appreciation Committee—which was the resonant title the four men had given their brotherhood—to rise up and depart the cozy flames and plunge down the briary mountainside in the dark, risking precious life and limb, to maybe catch a glimpse of the fox's brush disappearing or the possum's tail as bald as a rat's.

No-no. Their time-honored habit was to sit by the fire and pass a moderation jug of moon and listen to the singing of the hounds and watch the red sparks rise among the silver stars and jaw jaw jaw.

You can just hear them running on.

Old Pauley Mackail blips a sizzle of tobacco juice into the fire and continues his account of the bravest bear dog he's ever known, which was old Setback Williams's little dog, part bull and part feist and all mean, "and wasn't no bigger than a middling-size wharf rat, swear he wasn't. Ole Setback would bring his other fine dogs out on the leash, but this littlun, Whizzer was what they called him, he'd bring along in his jacket pocket. They'd find the scent and he'd turn the others loose, then he'd fetch little Whizzer out of his pocket and set him on the ground like a windup toy. Caught us by surprise every time; that dog was too little to remember. Touch his feet to the ground and he was gone from sight, didn't waste no time trailing by scent. Like he was part bear hisself if he wasn't only so little, and already knowed where the bear was laying at. Plumb disdained any help from the other dogs, go off and bring that bear to bay all by his lonesome; and could do it too, him being so fierce. He was so mean he shone out in the dark, a red-orangy glimmer in a dark room. EyeGod, I've seen him just like that in a hunting cabin at night many's the time." Then he folds his arms across his chest and leans back, daring the others to question his veracity.

They're too canny for that, seasoned hands at the campfire powwow.

"Whizzer, you say?" Broomsedge Tommy is talking now in his halt high-pitched twang, shifting his signature sprig of broomsedge to the side of his mouth. He's got a mean dog that tops old Pauley's; Tommy will always have a topper, but hard for him to get a story told, the way he flounders about in petty detail and soon sinks over his head. "Tillyard Crowe had him a dog so mean it one time took a bite out of Santy Claus. His name was Whizzer, too. . . . No wait now. Seems like he called him Wizard and not Whizzer. Because he had him this beagle bitch he called Witch, so he had him a Witch and a Wizard. . . . Maybe that's wrong, though, now I think. Might be Tillyard was the one had him one dog called Woolybooger and another one called Tallywhacker—"

So Wylie Hazel interrupts to tell his mean dog story because it has become obvious that Broomsedge Tommy is never going to reach the fascinating part of his account, the morbid attack on Santa Claus. Wylie chronicles Swann Dillard's German shepherd that was so mean and strong that Swann taught it to bite his logging chains in two and would've saved hisself a bait of money on boltcutters and hacksaws except that the dog got in the habit of crawling under the trucks and nibbling through the tie-rods.

And so forth and so on till the end of time.

My father rarely competed in the rivalries of quaint drollery. Maybe he felt outclassed. He lay stretched full out, his large square fleshy face propped on the heels of his hands. A handsome face, by most account, his boyish dimples and the humor crinkles of his middle years showing the tender alloy of his character. His eyes were dark gray but yellowed now by the fire he peered into, staring into the heart of the blaze as if some secret nested there, some message to tell him why the world he lived in must be so poky, so matter-of-fact, so lacking in spice.

He might rouse now and tell a mean dog stretcher that would cover his friends with scarlet shame, but to what purpose? It conferred no grand and permanent distinction to tell a whopping lie on the side of a mountain in western North Carolina in the pitch-dark. Derring-do was what was needed, some heroic feat that would en-

courage the spirits of hound dog men for generations to
come.

Then they all fell silent to hear the hounds way off in
the blackness. It sounded like they were down in a holler
somewhere to the left, and they were excited. Joe Robert
was no expert; he left the interpretation of these howls
and barks to the others. He didn't own a hunting dog,
and no longer even Queenie, our friendly collie who had
worked the cattle and patrolled the barns. He was a
member of the Committee only by courtesy. Hadn't paid
his dues yet this year. It cost an annual five hundred
dollars to belong to the Crazy Creek Wildlife Appreciation Committee, the money being refunded when a
member sighted his first fox of the year. So they each
reported spotting a fox while driving in to the first meeting. But my father had missed this initial get-together
and was in arrears that amounted to about two months'
worth of his school-teaching salary.

The music of the dogs was to him only cacophony, but
the others subjected this racket to as full a commentary
as ever a subtle monk wrung from the Book of Revela-
tions.

"There he goes," said Wylie Hazel. "There's old Blackfoot in the lead."

"Lead your grandmaw," Broomsedge Tommy said. "I
know that voice a hundred mile. That's my Stalker, just
a-gaining on that fox."

"It ain't no fox," Pauley Mackail said, "and it ain't no
Stalker. That's my Jollyboy on the scent of a coon. That
ain't the way they sound out after a fox. Not high-
pitched like that; fox runs em too hard."

"Now we're all wrong," Wylie said, "because Blackfoot has dropped off the lead and Greedygut has took it.
Can't you hear how they've changed over?" Only Wylie
had brought along two dogs this time, a distinct advan-

tage for braggartry. He threw back his head now and
gave out rending howls in imitation of his Greedygut.

They rattled on in this manner for a good long while
because, after all, it was the chase that heaped glory on
dog and master alike. Now it was that each man strove
to elicit admiration for the courage and strategy and vo-
cal accomplishment of his hound; yet each of them must
speak as if to trees and dumb stones, each so fascinated
with his own that he had no time even for charity toward other dogs. And since they never went to find out
the truth, each felt justified in his own magisterial opinion.

The strict order of this ritual irritated my father, and he
decided to poke a disorderly stick into the proceedings.

"Hush up, boys," he said. "Listen close now. Don't the
dogs sound real different tonight?"

They blinked. He'd been quiet so long they'd more or
less forgotten him. He had no dog, no stake in the chase.
Why was he talking at all?

"What you saying, Joe Robert?" Wylie Hazel asked.

"I say listen to them. Hear how excited they are?"

"You expect them to be excited," old Pauley said, "on
the scent of a coon."

"Fox," said Broomsedge Tommy Fowler.

"It's a different sound this time," my father said. "Listen close now."

Fresh volleys of pealing echoed out of the cove.

Broomsedge Tommy said, "They do sound a little different. They must be right on the heels of that fox."

"Coon," said old Pauley Mackail.

"Not but one time in my life," my father said, "did I
ever hear hounds sing out like they're doing now. This
was down east around White Lake and I was nothing
but a shirttail kid out hunting with some colored fellows
one night. And when they heard the hounds baying out

the way they are right now, they just looked at one another and shook their heads. Said it wouldn't be but one thing."

They gaped at my father, gaunt mountain faces expectant and credulous. They tended to credit stories about faraway places because they'd never traveled anywhere, and they would credit stories about Negroes because they'd rarely seen any. Of course, it came to them that Negroes had to be crackerjack hunters, coming from Africa where there were hordes of animals that made nothing but sunrise picnics of human beings.

"What did they say it was?" Wylie Hazel asked.

"They said it couldn't be anything else but a devil-possum."

"A possum-what?"

"Devil-possum. . . . Way I understand it, this is a whole different brand from our regular possums. I never did comprehend it all because they said there was voodoo mixed up in it. These devil-possums came out of the bayous down in Louisiana. Now your Louisiana bayou possum is an ugly mean sucker to begin with and then they got interbred with some kind of little old Mexican swamp bear. So they're half-possum half-bear but also tangled up with voodoo magic some way or another. I don't know the details about that, whether these voodoo people worship them or eat them or what. Some kind of voodoo power, is all I know."

"I never heard of nothing like that," Wylie said. "It sounds mighty damn silly."

"They're still pretty rare," my father said. "Don't find them that often even down in Louisiana. They're starting to spread out, though. There was a piece in the newspaper a little while back about how they've been spotted in South Carolina and north Georgia."

That impressed them, the devil-possum in the papers.

Old Pauley said he hadn't read about nothing like that, but they discounted his testimony because he'd never read a newspaper but one time and then he'd got the facts boozled up. Unless Canada really had declared war on Australia and modern history was keeping the fact secret.

"I ain't believing no devil-possum," Wylie said. "I ain't believing the first word."

"No hide off my ass what you don't believe," my father said. "I'm just telling you what-all I've heard."

"Well, if there *was* some kind of demon-possum like that—I mean, just supposing—what would he do to the dogs?"

Did they hear now an undertone of real apprehension in Wylie's question?

"It wouldn't be pretty," my father said. "As soon as those fellows knew what it was, they called their dogs back."

"Aw, Wylie," Pauley Mackail said, "this is just some big jacktale Joe Robert is telling us."

"Yeah, I know. Only old Blackfoot and Greedygut are the best hunting dogs that ever lived in the world."

"They ain't so almighty much," Broomsedge Tommy said. "But if anything was to happen to Stalker, I believe it would be the death of me."

My father said, "All I can tell you is that this devil-possum has no more fear of making a dog's close acquaintance than a flea does."

"Well, tell us what he looks like," Wylie said. "I can't seem to get no clear picture."

"All I've got to go by is what other folks tell me, people who've seen it," my father said. "And they report that he's about three to four times bigger than your regular possum and of a light tan color with black spots."

"Like a black and tan hound?" Broomsedge Tommy asked.

"Huh-uh. Round spots, round as polka dots. And he's strong. Long claws, so he can zip to the top of a tree before you can say your proper name. Teeth. Teeth as long as a bear's, that's the Mexican in him. But the strangest thing is, he's got a face mighty like a human face. I reckon this is the voodoo part, that he's got a face like a little old man."

"An old man's face?" Wylie said.

"With whiskers and a big bristly mustache."

"A big mustache?"

"And sideburns," my father said. He was getting into the swing of it now. "Frizzy muttonchop sideburns."

"Let me see if I've got it straight what this thing looks like," Wylie Hazel said. "This here *possum* is black and yellow polka-dotted with long ugly claws and teeth and has got a face like a little old man with whiskers and mustaches and muttonchop sideburns. . . . Now are there any other distinctive markings? Because I wouldn't want to go out hunting and shoot a sheep or chicken by mistake."

"Well, maybe the eyes."

"What about the eyes?"

"They say they're a bright yellow-green and they flame out at you in the dark."

"All right," Wylie said. "I will add on to your description yellow eyes that shine like car headlights. That ought to stop me from plugging my mother-in-law by mistake. Because the rest of it matches up with her pretty well."

"I'm just saying what I've been told."

Old Pauley broke in. "You think that's what the dogs

have got treed? Because they've got something up in the air. Just listen to them."

"I hope they ain't treed my mother-in-law," Wylie said. "She'll tear em apart."

Along the spiky ridges, under the cool stars, rang out the mournful quavers and semiquavers and sobbing caesuras to proclaim that the pursued, whatever species it belonged to, had found a tree to settle in like a fairy-tale princess in a tower, while the pursuers like plaintive troubadours serenaded from below.

"See there?" my father said. "You never heard them sound like that before."

"I don't hear them sound no different," Wylie said.

"Seems like they do sound a little different," Tommy said. He spat a frazzle of broomsedge at the fire, took another toothpick-sized joint of it from his overalls bib, and fitted it into the corner of his mouth.

Wylie snorted. "You'd believe any damn thing, Tommy. I wisht I was a gold mine salesman to come knocking on your door."

"All I can tell you is what I know from a long time ago," my father said.

A long time ago. He was choosing phrases to work upon their imaginations. He was perfectly satisfied it was a possum the dogs had treed down there in the holler— or a coon. What difference did it make? . . . And rather than loll here and listen to yammer about whether the dogs had treed a coon or a possum and which one of the dogs had made scent first and which one was leading the pack and whether the refuge tree was a persimmon or a chestnut, rather than all this useless heated fil-ibuster, why not go down yonder and collar that possum and take him home? There'd be lots of situations where a possum would come in handy. Seemed like his fam-ily—his tartly tolerant wife, his strict religious mother-in-law, his weirdly studious son, his sunny blond four-year-old daughter—needed a jolt now and then, needed jarring up a bit. Otherwise they'd get set in their ways and Joe Robert Kirkman would become bored and then if he wasn't careful, he'd be finding mischief to get into.

And so he said: "One way to settle it. Let's go see what they've got treed."

Wylie Hazel's mouth dropped in astonishment. He couldn't seem to close it.

"Hike down into the holler and have a look," my father said.

Old Pauley Mackail stared at him so hard his eyes crossed.

"Take us a little look-see," my father said. "Where's the harm in that?"

Tommy clutched at his throat. In sudden overwhelming amazement, he had sucked down his sprig of broomsedge.

"I've got this certain hunch it's a devil-possum," my father said. "I'll wager five hundred dollars it's him sitting up there in the tree."

"Then you'd owe the Appreciation Committee an even thousand," Wylie said. "And no way can you see your first fox of the year two times."

"It's a mighty strong hunch I've got."

"Well hell then, let's go," Wylie said. "Tommy, fetch that lantern there so we can see. Pauley, you bring along your .45 pistol. We will probably want to shoot this booger-coon and get it stuffed for our great-grand-children to wonder at."

Old Pauley and Tommy said all right and the four men set off.

But it's not easy to find where the dogs are located out in the shaggy mountains in the dark—especially if you've lost the knack of trailing them, out of practice for

twelve years and more. Down in the hollers there between one hogback ridge and another, the sound of baying seems to come from all directions at once. There are
blind coves with slick and snaky ledges, old dry creekbeds that don't lead anywhere and other creekbeds not
dry at all. There are thickets so dense you feel like you've
been popped into the black iron washpot and the lid
clapped over your head.

They were sorely disused, but after a while some of the
old habits began to reassert themselves. Wylie Hazel uttered profanities he could barely remember, and old
Pauley Mackail resurrected swear words probably un-
heard since Kentucky rifles fired upon British redcoats.
But while exciting language served somewhat to vent
their emotions, it did nothing to prevent trippings and
tumbles, falls, spills, and somersaults; and it was no balm
for bruises, cuts, contusions, and punctures. The mountain gave its guests a sound pummeling this aye night.

Still they pursued the music of the dogs, leaping and
floundering and gasping and bleeding and sweating,
with three of the four of them vowing secret terrible re-
venges upon my father's head.

At last they reached the tree, more than a little surprised to do so. They felt they'd actually only blundered
upon the medium-sized poplar with the hounds in
heated debate at the foot of it, the dogs vaulting upward
toward the mystery hidden in the leaves like the thirsty
souls of prophets attempting to penetrate the nature of
God.

Then the dogs stopped jumping about and fell absolutely silent. They had noticed the presence of their mas-
ters, come for the first time in living memory to the scene
of the encounter. They were dumbfounded and you
could read from the expressions on their faces what they
thought, Greedygut saying, What the hell are these guys

here for? and Jollyboy saying, We must have come plumb round in a circle, and Blackfoot saying, If this don't beat all I ever seen, and Stalker, Hold me up, boys, I think I'm having a heart attack.

Then Broomsedge Tommy bawled out, "Go get em, Stalker," and the dogs shook off their astonishment and resumed their concert.

"Boys, we made it," old Pauley said. "I wasn't sure I could do it no more."

"Aw now, Mackail," my father said, "you're not an old man yet."

"Well then, I'm disappointed," he said, "because I've sure worked at it long enough."

They all sat down and panted awhile. The ground was damp and smelled of moss and humus and subterranean waters. The starry sky stretched so close over the cove it looked like a holey tent roof. The men looked up into the tree, into the shifting black cave of new leaves. They could see nothing.

"This here tree's too big to shake him out," Wylie said. "If we're going to catch him, we'll have to go up. What you think, Tommy?"

"Ain't but one way to do it," said Broomsedge Tommy. "Skin up this nice poplar."

"If you don't mind, boys, I'm going to back off of this chore," old Pauley said.

"All right then," my father said. "Who's man enough to climb this tree?"

They smiled smug smiles then and the three of them turned and fixed upon my father a serene and level gaze.

So at three in the morning of a May day in 1946, he was struggling up a menacing poplar, fixing to bring back alive the fabled deadly devil-possum, which he had only just finished fabricating out of thin air. He wore a thick cotton shirt and a pair of stout denim trousers he was grateful for. A roll of seagrass twine was tucked into his shirt pocket and tied to a belt loop.

There was a critter of some kind in this tree and Joe Robert Kirkman was going to spit in its eye, grab it by the scruff of the neck, and cram it into the totesack he was carrying in his teeth. The heady taste of dirty burlap filled his senses. Up he went, slowly and raggedly, but receiving plenty of encouragement from below. Here was Stalker baying Hooo, and Greedygut howling Hoowoo, and Jollyboy yapping Weep weep weep weep weep, and Blackfoot barking Riprap riprap riprap. His comrades, too, were urging him to gird his loins for conflict. Broomsedge Tommy shouts, "Let's see you grab that five-hundred-dollar devil-possum, Joe Robert," and Wylie Hazel hollers, "Don't let that possum pull no voodoo hoodoo," and old Pauley says, "Rassle him down, we'll have a devil-possum breakfast."

It was a thrilling space of time for my father, perhaps a bit more thrilling than he'd bargained for, and he was glad to gain the first fair-sized limb and slide over onto it and sit there for a minute or two and catch his breath. He'd climbed up about fifteen feet now.

He peered uneasily among the leaves and branches, black against the night sky. He tried to listen, but all he could hear was the tarnation racket below, the men and dogs raving up at him like lunatics. Nothing he could do about that. He looked, but whatever coon or possum was in this tree would surely be higher, near the very top.

Up he went again, scratching and knocking his hands and head in the dark, though Lord knows he'd had plenty of practice climbing trees. He'd once worked two long years for the Carolina Power and Light Company, clearing land to install power lines through the ruggedest part of the mountains. He'd grubbed out bushes and topped trees and cut them down, and now you could travel down past Harmon Den and Laurel Fork and up through Betsey's Gap and see the inexorable alien march of towers over slope and ridge and rockface, the heavy lines swooping between them, bringing scientific electrical illumination to fleabite settlements in the mountains, where such light had never been heard of before.

So he'd climbed plenty of trees, but this was a different proposition, squirming up in the dark to lay hands on an unseen animal, with a loud convocation of insanity taking place below. Many separate things were going on at once, and when my father realized this, he decided to slow down and tread easy. Better not to get all flustered. He had climbed up about twenty-five feet now, and the branches were not much thicker than pencils, and the slender trunk began to sway, and many stars pierced through the leaves. And still he didn't see anything—and then he did.

He thought he did.

Maybe there was something dark in the dark, perched out on a limb slightly above him. Seemed to be about eight feet away and seemed to be an uncomfortably large raccoon. Could those dim yellow lights be eyes? The totesack began to suffocate him and he took it out of his mouth and held it in his right hand. Then he slipped the coil of twine from his pocket and let it dangle to the bottom. He hoped they were taking notice down there that he needed the lantern.

He climbed quietly until he was level in the tree with his prey and precariously balanced on two little limbs about five feet from it. Thirty feet up. The dark creature didn't shift an inch.

There was a tug on the line, and Joe Robert began to draw the lantern up, careful not to snag it in the branches. It was eerie to watch the yellow-orange glow rise toward him, the bell jar of light lapping like an echo over the men and dogs and bushes and leaf-strewn ground. A silent and angelic vision, the flame ascending to his feet and legs, brightening only him and gradually darkening all the world it left behind.

He caught the lantern by the bail and lifted it chest-high. Steadied his feet as best he could and took up the totesack. He extended the lantern little by little toward the waiting shape of darkness.

Then he wished he had never climbed into this mid-night tree and he wished—with the cold sweat pouring off him all over—that he'd never told a lie, not even the most harmless fib, in all his life.

Also he cried out, "Lord Jesus, forgive us if You can!" A phrase that would stick in his craw for months to come.

For there, enthroned on a limb not three feet away, sat the genuine and undeniable devil-possum just as my father had described the monster.

One trouble was that he had described his patchwork terror without truly imagining it, merely flinging silly words about. He hadn't the least thought what it would be like to actually *see* the beast, which really was dotted yellow-and-black, which really did have fearsome long claws and teeth, whose great yellow-green eyes shone like emeralds in the lantern light. Indeed it did look like a sardonic and mocking little old man with long coarse mustachios and white muttonchop sideburns and a short but recognizable goatee. And which, moreover, spat a crackling sibilant phrase of unknown language at my father and gave an offhand but malicious swipe at his lantern.

Wherefore: *O Lord Jesus, forgive us if You can!*

The vehemence of his utterance and the profundity of

its sentiment suddenly and entirely quelled the melee at the foot of the tree. The men fell silent and the dogs, too, and they peered up anxiously, mouths open like coffee mugs.

Broomsedge Tommy shouted, "Are you all right, Joe Robert? When it looks too dangerous, come on down."

If my father heard this piece of advice, he must have considered it superfluous, since his natural human fright, coupled with the devil-possum's powerful blow, had caused him to misstep and he was already falling out of the tree at a middling rate of speed. The resilient branches of the poplar did slow him down, though, and he had opportunity for an interesting variety of impulses, memories, impressions, and odd thoughts.

In the first 2.7 seconds of his falling, the answer to the riddle of human existence flashed into his mind, the idea that had eluded all the passionate philosophers from Socrates to Heidegger. But unfortunately the excitement of the moment blotted the important discovery from my father's mind and he was never able to recall it.

It then occurred to him that he might try to do something to save his life. Here he was, falling out of a tree while clutching a burning lantern in his left hand and a filthy totesack in his right. Maybe one of these pieces of equipment could be useful—but which one? It wasn't a closely reasoned choice, but he decided to drop the lantern. It tumbled among the branches and fell in a line parallel to the tree trunk, illuminating as it fell the animal my father had frightened from its perch and which now leapt headfirst down the trunk, following so closely the flight of the lantern, it seemed to be trying to catch up with it. When they touched ground together, the lantern went out and was lost in the bushes and the beast went swoosh and was gone forever.

Wylie Hazel shouted up, "Durn your eyes, Joe Robert, that ain't no devil-possum. It's a damn big bobcat."

But my father, still busily falling out of the tree, did not reply to this grievance, pondering with avid attention some aspects of the problem of life and death. In these last few years, he had seen, like everyone else, many newsreel sequences of paratroopers leaping from airplanes and floating to earth easy as thistledown. And he wished his old totesack would open like a parachute and let him down gently. . . . Then he was amused to observe what frail straws a man's mind will clutch at in his anxious hours. . . . Then he noticed that he was not only thinking thoughts during these harried moments, he was also subjecting them to critical and aesthetic judgments. He had discovered a universal law, one that he felt ought to be enshrined in the physics textbooks along with those of Galileo, Pascal, and Newton: *A man falling in space toward the nearest center of gravity will be attacked by a whole bunch of foolish notions.* It was an imprecise formulation, but it would have to do for the time being.

The totesack did not exactly oblige. That is, it did not open like a cartoon umbrella to waft my father silkily down to earth. But it did snag securely on the stub of a broken limb and swing him against the trunk. He hit the tree hard with his shoulder and the left side of his face but managed to wrap his left arm around the trunk, and then his sore right arm. He held on tight and slid to the ground as if sliding down a barbarous fireman's pole.

He sat flat on the ground with his arms around the tree and he wouldn't let go. He felt battered, painful, triumphant, silly, relieved, embarrassed, and filled with a grateful piety. If she could have known, my grandmother would have been pleased with the high religious tone of his cogitation.

They had to pry him loose one finger at a time, he had such devoted regard for that tree trunk. There were no dogs to get in the way because they'd set out instantly after the bobcat, which they didn't know any better than to catch up with, until it wheeled about and gave them a choleric piece of its mind and scattered them to the points of the compass. Two weeks would pass before the four dogs were recovered from separate counties.

Meanwhile, they had peeled my father loose from the tree. They made him stand up and he was pleased and amazed to be able to do it.

"How you feeling?" Wylie asked.

"All right, I guess. A little sore on my left-hand side."

"I can understand that," Wylie said.

"How do I look?"

"Tell you the truth, Joe Robert, you appear to be pretty well banged up. You won't win no beauty prizes for the next few days."

"I'm sorry to hear it," my father said. "I need to look my best today."

"How come?" asked old Pauley.

"I've got a meeting with the governor of North Carolina this afternoon. If my looks suit him, I've got a chance at a high-paying job and the use of a Cadillac car."

They could only gape at him.

Finally, Broomsedge Tommy asked, "Is that the truth, Joe Robert? The governor?"

Surely at this moment there must have been a voice of dread authority in the back of his mind that spoke to him and said: Joe Robert Kirkman, if you don't stop propagating these intolerable falsehoods, the next time there in the top of a tree on the top of a mountain at four o'clock in the morning, it'll be a purple man-eating gorilla sent to keep you company.

"Of course, it's the truth," my father said. "I wouldn't tell you boys a lie. The truth is sacred to me."

The truth was, in fact, so sacred to my father that he generally refused to profane its sanctity with his worldly presence.

Two

MORNING

ABLUTIONS

It was still dark when my father got home at 4:30 in the morning. He pulled the blue Ford pickup into the yard, parked beneath the walnut tree, and cut the headlights. For a minute or two, he sat still, thinking, listening to the motor heat tick out of the hood metal and to the silence that gathered around this insectile little noise.

What's this? Nobody awake yet? Nobody to welcome the doughty hunter? They're going to sleep their lives away, my father thought. I wish I'd caught that bobcat.

Let him loose in the house, he'd give em a pepper re-
veille.

He opened the door and got out but—*oww*—it hurt to
stir. He eased down to sit on the running board and
massaged his neck and left shoulder. No bones broken.
He thought he could get through the day all right, but
the pain was bad and he didn't want to think what he
must look like. It was a misfortune to be uglied up; he
really did have an important meeting this afternoon. Not
with the governor of North Carolina and all his Cadillac
cars, but with a group of tedious people who had in
mind to fire him from his job, rob him of his livelihood,
and exile his innocent soul to Cimmerian darkness. But
my father had planned to keep his guard up; he was
going to bear himself meekly and say No *sir* and Yes
ma'am and look sharp and shiny in his one good suit. He
was going to sell them a heart-wrenching poor-mouth
fairy tale. And now just look at him, all banged up top to
bottom and with a doubtlessly spectacular black eye.
They would only conclude that he had spent the midnight hours slugging it out with his hoodlum friends in
the honky-tonks.

Well, let them think whatever minuscule notions they
were capable of forming. Wait till they heard what he
thought about where they stood in relation to the civilized society of the twentieth century.

No-no. Settle down, Joe Robert, he told himself. Smile
and slide easy—that's the policy. Got to protect the family, ease into a step or two of the Soft-shoe Hypocrite
Shuffle.

He stood up, but the dark silence of my grandmother's
house defeated him, and the tiresome prospect of trying
to explain the way he looked. Now that he thought,
there was no good reason to be rousting his family from

their beds. No need to search out trouble that was already looking for him.

He decided to head on out to the barns and do the morning chores. There was plenty of time, so he'd let Jess sleep in. Let him dream those incomprehensible dreams completely out of his head; let him wake up late then, having become as sane and sensible as his father. Fat chance. Joe Robert felt certain in his heart that he would never understand his son and would always live uneasy with him.

He went into the little milk room in back of the side porch. It was chilly and damp in there with the thick whitewashed plaster walls and the spring-fed cement trough that kept the ten-gallon steel milk cans cool and healthy. Odors of clean water and earth, with a slight spicing of soured milk. He sat in a butt-sprung cane chair and took off his hunting boots and pulled on his barn shoes, heavy-caked soft-smelling brogans. Jammed a lumpy gray felt hat low over his brow and slipped into a foul corduroy jacket that seemed never to have seen better days. This outfit my mother called his "working clothes," but he named it his Peasant Costume. "Every time I get into these duds," he said, "it makes me want to overthrow the Czar." He grabbed a milk pail and a big steel can and went out.

He loved the short walk to the barn over the crackling gravel road in the warm spring morning with the stars white and blue and yellow in the sky like a bowl of delirium and the apple trees on the right-hand hill moving and whispering and Trivet Creek in the left-hand bottom fields shining in the dim light like steel braid. Now came the faintest tinge of dawn, just enough to give smooth scallop outline to the eastern hills and hard angular outline to the three barns. His mornings began with this walk and he looked forward to it all night in his sleep.

In the grassy glacis between the first two barns, he stopped to take a leak. The grass was short here and my father was pissing his initials on the hillside, ambitious to set dark green letters lush against the paler green background. He had almost finished a recognizable hook for the J, but this effort had taken five weeks. He rebuttoned his fly, thinking, Take heed, world, Joe Robert Kirkman will make his mark, you'll see.

He went into the lower crib of the first barn and shucked six ears of corn to divide between the horses and went out and dropped them into the stall troughs along with four handfuls of dry feed. As always, Jackson and Maude muttered to one another, nodding over their breakfast. They were a famous pair of talkers, these two, with a penchant for metaphysics. "Tomorrow we three will be in the bottom, plowing corn," my father told them. "Ha." Let em mull that over; they both hated to plow on Saturday.

So did he, come to that.

He pulled some weeds and tossed them into the pigpen. Eve, the old sow, didn't bother to rise, but the four shoats—Matthew, Mark, Luke, and John—scampered to the greenery and snuffled. Custom averred that it was bad luck to name animals that were to be killed and eaten, but my father had declared eternal war upon custom. He had a talent for names and would bestow them even upon trees and cornstalks that caught his attention. As, for example, that suggestive young sassafrass bush on the hill that he called Rita Hayworth. . . . Later Jess would feed the pigs kitchen slop and shorts mixed with a little raw milk—if he ever got out of bed.

Then he went into the milking barn. This was a low

mean dark little room under the road-level loft. He lit
the lantern that hung by the door and fixed it on a nail
in a middle joist, where it illuminated redly the straw-
and-manure-caked floor, the ceiling baggy with dust-
wooly cobweb, the narrow board stalls with their deep
feed troughs. Warm shadows moved when he moved. It
was close in there, but he rather liked the sweet-sour
smell of manure and trampled hay and warm cow. There
was a comfort in it that he carried somewhere in his
head all day long. In two of the stalls, he dumped
ground corn, shelled corn, and a sprinkling of cottonseed
meal. Then he crossed to the door to the cow lot and
opened it.

The cows were dark against the brightening east. They
ambled in as slow as seasons coming on, pausing in the
lantern glow for a moment, lifting their heads so that
their melting brown eyes glowed orange. They went
readily to their stalls, Daphne and Big Red and Minerva
and Wanderlust and Daisy and Little Red, and my father
went round and clipped the stall chains to their neck
halters. He had fed Minerva and Little Red, and he took
down the three-legged stool and grabbed a pail and began milking.

Now wasn't this the sweetest part of the day, milking
the easy cows? Nudging head and shoulder into the
comforting flanks, washing the teats and squeezing them
gently at first in case of soreness and gradually building
into rhythm, stream after straight stream in a pulse as
regular as the stately heart of the animal, bright jets of
milk Xing to fill the pail with warm lace, with delicate
foam that touched his knuckles like a spiderweb. These
days, these hours, were of life the cream supreme, wrestling devil-possums in the midnight stars and peeing
your name in the grass and milking cows. . . . But then
he felt on the back of his neck the hungry accusing gaze

of Sherlock the barn cat and he shifted on his stool and
squirted six quick arrows of milk upon his chest. In a
graceful, if rather finical manner, Sherlock wiped his
dripping fur and licked the milk foam from his right
paw, lip-lip, lip-lip.

He went from one to another. Like a big old Daddy
Bee, he thought, visiting his big old Mama Roses. Then
he went round again to strip the last drops; didn't want
them to go dry. Four times he emptied his pail into the
five-gallon can.

He unclipped their chains and drove them through the
lot and across the road by the other barn and let down
the three long pine poles that barred the pasture. As they
filed through, he said, "All right, ladies, don't forget to
punch the time clock." Dew shrouded the hills of grass
and in the early light the pasture looked like a landscape
of heaped laundry. "Wish I was going with you," he
said. "Wish I could hang out all day and eat cool grass."
And he actually imagined himself doing so, and figured
that he would be good at it.

He returned to the milking barn and got his pail and
the heavy warm steel can. He stood for a moment now,
looking about and remembering. This was the place
where he and Jess and Johnson Gibbs had once run
afoul of divine revelation, where almighty God had spoken to Joe Robert, telling him something he could understand for a blessed change. It was my father's opinion
that God was something of a windbag, continually talking to mankind, but pitching His discourse beyond our
abbreviated human capacities. His method was too op-
timistic, and God lost most of His audience. My father
remembered that his physics professor at Acton College
had much the same difficulty.

The walk back to the house with the heavy can was
less exciting than the earlier walk, but it was still fine.

The sky had whitened and it looked to be a cloudless day coming on, bright and warm, maybe a little fog along the river when the air heated. The morning was beginning to ferment, birds tuning up by the sliding creek yonder, and this Friday had opportunity to become a generous and elegant day.

Except that he had to lose part of it on some grunty narrow-minded flinthearts who were after his hide.

But what the hell. These difficulties were part of the job, an inevitable part of life.

No.

Not in his book.

He figured it this way: When you kept a willing heart, an open mind, you saw life as a collocation of extremities. On one side were terror, despair, catastrophe, tragic ruin, and flood and famine and torture and disease. Humanity had just fought a war of such soul-harrowing proportion that only the first installment of Armageddon could bring it to an end. On the other side were Nature in her every aspect, brutal or smiling, and a persistent smolder of kindliness in the greater mass of mankind. There were stars and animals and trees and microbes; there were women to love and friends who lived and died and other people, too, who said and did the goofiest things imaginable. There was a lovely quiet in the midst of hilarious turmoil. There was, in short, the flashing phantasmagoria of rational life, the wild endearing circus of sense and circumstance. This life is the Big Time—what shining sage uttered those words? Grasp the yardstick of existence anywhere along its length, take it up with an attitude of happy disinterest, and see if the extremities, horror and joy, despair and contentment, were not ends of the same standard, and composed of the very same materials. Take away the stuff of tears, there is nothing left to make laughter of.

Man did not come to this planet merely to mark time. You never had simply to endure, to put up with.

Except—when sometimes you did.

This was my father, the Moral Philosopher, who, in thinking these thoughts, considered that he was merely marking time.

In the milk room, he poured the morning's harvest into the twenty-gallon can, washed the smaller can and the pail and the strainer cloths and hung these to dry. He changed out of the peasant outfit, then rolled an easy Prince Albert cigarette and sat down. He pretended that in these moments of leisure he was planning the day to come, and so he was. He arranged it all in his head in sensible order and then forgot it all as soon as he rose from the chair.

He entered the main house, all silent and dark. In the hall bathroom, he washed up and brushed his teeth and shaved as best he could, but this was no simple job, the left side of his face scratched and lumpy and purpling. The left eye was a rainbow epic.

He went into his bedroom and changed clothes again, putting on his good gray Sunday-go-to-meeting suit, the only truly presentable suit he owned. He combed his hair tentatively in the dark mirror. He didn't snap the light on because Cora was still asleep. On his tiptoe way out of the room, he paused to look down at my mother warm in the sheets. Sleep on, Sleeping Beauty, he thought, I'll fix my own breakfast.

Before he went into the kitchen, he climbed the stairs and looked in on my sister and me. She slept across the room in the bed I used to occupy and I slept now in the tall bed that had been Johnson Gibbs's. Easy to recognize the tender smiling gaze he gave my sister. Mitzi was four years old and blondly adorable and she was his sunshine, his only sunshine, who made him happy when skies were gray. About me, he was less certain his whole life long and it must have been with a baffled curiosity that he looked at me there, a tumble of fool in a blanket, the bed cluttered with books and the floor around strewn with them. Probably he picked up the translation of Vergil I was reading, thumbed through and gently replaced it. Probably he thought a thought then that wouldn't occur to him again for months or years. He shook his head slowly before pulling the door closed and going downstairs.

I slept on, never waking ever in my life, dreaming of the man who battled the devil-possum and the false prophet and the forces of dark ignorance. I dreamed, too, of Aeneas carrying his father on his shoulders toward the shores of the future. I dreamed of ilex and osier and of the honeybees that were the souls of all the dead.

My father was a culinary cataclysm of grand magnitude. He fancied, of course, that he was a fine cook, that he could build a tasty meal out of discardable orts, that he knew what was proper for the human body, and that he had a certain touch, the old *je ne sais quoi.*

But first off, he dropped the egg he was washing into the sink. It took a few minutes to gather the bits of shell, slide them off his hands into the slop bucket, and wipe the sink with a fresh tea towel. Why was he washing an egg that he was going to scramble? I'd better be careful, he thought, I don't want to spot my good suit, not today. Then he decided he preferred French toast, so he broke another egg on a serving platter and plopped in a slice of bread and poked it around with his finger. The coffee water was boiling and he burned his hand lifting the kettle with its iron handle. When he hoisted the gooey bread from the platter toward the smoking frying pan, it tore apart and splashed egg on his vest. He wet another tea towel and dabbed at the fabric. Doesn't look too bad, he thought. Nobody'll notice.

In thirty minutes, he had finished breakfast. That was a triumph. He had eaten all of his cooking that he could endure, and he had escaped with his life. The kitchen, though, had not escaped; every surface, including much of the ceiling, was colorful with drip, spatter, and smear. Shards of glass, eggshell, and crockery were piled on the corner of the dining table. There was disaster of every sort, including a sink that would retain its power to disgust for weeks to come. There was evident everywhere the hand of reckless genius.

But my father simply did not recognize this cyclopean shambles. He looked round the ruined room and thought, There's nothing like a man's touch with breakfast; the womenfolk could learn a trick or two.

Outside it was morning at last. The sun was perched like a goldfinch on the rim of the mountains, the sky was silver, blue, the birds assaulted the hour with full-throated joy. He had thirty miles to drive to school and was glad for the brightness.

Before he climbed into the pickup, he turned to gaze at the house. "Well, family," he said, "thanks for the company and the scintillating conversation. I don't know when I've met a livelier bunch." Wait till tonight at supper. He'd guy them unmercifully; they'd never sleep late again.

Then he got in and drove off toward his working day.

He didn't get far before something else happened.

The gravel road that connected our farm to the paved streets of Tipton and then to all the other highways of the world ran parallel to Trivet Creek for about five miles. Trivet was no swift deep creek, just an ordinary mountain meander, until it reached Piggot's dam just above the place where it joined the black and chemically foul Pigeon River. Above the dam, though, it was slow and deep until it spilled flashing over the top. Old Piggot and his four grim daughters used to work a grain mill here, but Piggot was long gone from the earth and his daughters scattered and the big unmoving iron wheel stood alone, the mill house all tumbled down. But the dam remained, with its smooth millrace.

In this deep water, my father spotted someone struggling for dear life.

At first, he didn't think it was anyone, and he thought, Is that a loghead or a turtle? He took a closer look and, sure enough, it was a person fighting the current with a terrible lack of success. It was a child in the water there.

He braked the truck into the muddy ditch and killed the motor and tumbled out. He vaulted over the barbwire fence and ran thrashing through the wet weeds to the bank. Was it—? Yes, it was a child, male or female he couldn't tell, trying weakly to swim upstream away from the dam, making no headway, and, in fact, just at that moment sinking like a soaked rag doll.

The ground was mushy on the grassy lip of the bank and he teetered wildly, tearing off his jacket, before diving into the stream. He gapsed in pain, as much at the shock of the icy water as at the agony of his injured left arm as he brought it forward swimming. Where was the child? He raised his head and shook the water out of his eyes, but for a few moments he could see nothing and he was afraid that he was too late. Then he saw the victim—*just under the water*—about fifteen yards away and he swam clumsily, grindingly. He changed his stroke to a less painful dog paddle.

He had made up his mind to rescue this kid and was determined, too, that he wouldn't drown. His death would spoil all the gallantry of the gesture, and the only advantage in it would be to make irrelevant the damage to his only good suit. He was thinking almost entirely of his suit just at that moment when he grasped the child by the shirt collar and began to pull toward safety.

It wasn't easy. He was beginning to tire and the cold water hadn't dulled the pain in his left side as he had hoped it would. The pain was like burning iron, and swimming back was like crawling uphill through an avalanche. When he reached the edge, he spiked his heels into the mud and leaned into the bank to hold himself there to breathe and to lift the child's head above the water. He rested for a minute or so, then squirmed round and wormed his way up, digging in with his elbows and hoping that his grip on the shirt collar wasn't strangling the little fellow.

He gained the top of the bank and rolled himself and the child into the safety of the long grass and lay there for a moment heaving and coughing. He rose to his knees. He was exhausted and blue with cold and he could think only that he had to get the water out of the child's lungs and he prayed that the pulmonary exercise he had taught so often in his Boy Scout First Aid classes actually worked. To tell the truth, he'd always felt silly showing off that push-rest-push business.

It was a little girl. He turned her on her stomach. She would be eight, maybe nine, years old, with short dark hair. She was wearing a white cotton shirt with piped collar and sleeves and blue jeans, a cowgirl outfit. Lucky the buttons hadn't popped off that shirt; she would have dropped to the bottom and he could never have dredged her up, too weak and wounded.

Just as he began the resuscitation procedure, she belched a gush of dark water and blinked her eyes. Hey-hey, it was wonderful. Nothing I do now, he thought, will kill her. I'll get my merit badge even if I don't do this drill exactly right. He rolled her over again and placed his hands across the small of her back and began to pump.

He was amazed to find that the method worked. Water dribbled out of her mouth and nose and she coughed wracked sobs. He let her go and she turned to face him and asked in a pitiable small voice, "Mister, what are you doing?" Then she passed out.

He turned her over once more and began again. "Well, little girl, I'm in the process of saving your life, at great bother and expense to me. Don't you think I'm going to forget it, either. After you grow up and marry an oil well millionaire and I'm a decrepit old bankrupt with snaggledy teeth, I'll come to your front door expecting a pension." He punctuated his phrases with the prescribed exertions. "But if you take and die on me, well, don't expect to see my sweet face again."

In a few minutes, she regained consciousness, hacking and snuffling. Her lips were blue-black and her face white as Kleenex and her eyes red and teary, but she looked better. She looked alive; and though my father always maintained that he envied dead people their sinecure positions in the world, he actually preferred the living, who responded so much more immediately to his jokes.

She was suffering from the cold. So was he, come to that. "Wait," he said. "Hold on a minute." He rose weakly and went to retrieve his serge jacket. It was all damp and covered with seeds and weed leaves. He took it back and wrapped it round the little girl and lifted her and began stumbling toward the truck. His teeth chattered and his left arm throbbed powerfully. He wrestled through the weeds to the fence and tried to cross it gracefully, thinking he might prevent the final ruin of his suit. No mercy here: snagged a dozen times.

He slid her into the truck cab and went round and got in. His rear-left wheel was in the gravel—that was one piece of good luck—and he started off toward succor and comfort.

The heater was feeble when it worked at all, but he turned it on. She crouched under his jacket, wild-eyed and shuddering. She was an awfully peaked little thing, he thought; then reflected that he probably didn't favor a movie star himself right now. Her eyes were large and dark and lost, and my father thought of his own Mitzi, his little golden girl. What if she fell in Trivet and drowned? He would lay down rules tonight about where Mitzi could and could not wander. Jess, too. Lord knows, anything could happen these days. Just look at her huddled in the seat, her teeth chattering like a hay rake on a rocky road.

"How're you feeling, honey?"

She could only stare out into the mist beginning to rise from the creek. He peered more carefully, too, slowing a little. He asked her name, but she couldn't answer that, either. No matter. The main thing was to get warm, the both of them.

He came to the asphalt intersection of the road that led to the left by the Challenger Paper and Fiber Company into the mouse-colored town of Tipton. On his right was a patched iron bridge across Trivet and, nudged in below it, in the fork where Trivet joined the gooey black despoiled Pigeon River, sat Virgil Campbell's Gro.

Which was now named on the sign as the Bound for Hell Grocery & Dry Goods, the proprietor alluding to a joke no one remembered. My father had been praying it wasn't too early for opening hours, or that Virgil hadn't decided to give this Friday over to whiskey; he needed the fire in that potbelly stove.

He pulled into the sloped gravelway and got out and tried the door. The place was open, but he couldn't see anyone inside. The four naked overhead bulbs lit dimly the grimy oiled aisles and the tables and gloomy shelves.

"Virgil? Anybody here?"

There was a muffled rustle in the back. "Who the hell wants to know?"

"Show some merciful charity," my father said. "You've got two people here on the verge of extinction."

The shrewd and alarmingly scarlet face of Virgil Campbell, with its thatch of silvery cotton candy hair, appeared over a counter piled with bolts of dimity, gingham, chintz. "Top of the mornin'," he said.

"Have you got a fire going?" my father asked. "We're in desperate need of a fire."

"I'm blowing on it," Virgil said, "but it's a slow go. I ain't got the lungs no more of a woolyworm."

"Keep on puffing. I'll bring in our drowning victim." He went to the truck. When he looked at the little girl, she turned upon him a gaze so sad and sick that a dread pity came over him like the shadow of a tombstone. He gathered her up, tucking the jacket round her, and carried her into the back of the store, where Virgil was feeding the small flutter of blaze with kindling.

When he peeped up at my father and saw the child, he said, "Gawd-a-mighty," and scurried off and returned with a pint of turpentine. "Stand away," he said and poured out the whole bottle, jumping back as the flames shot up into the stovepipe and licked out the door, giving off a smell of piny woods. He threw in a double handful of kindling. "We've got us one now," he said.

"Good."

He nodded at the child. "What you got there?"

"I found her in the creek," my father said. "Whose do you reckon she is?"

"She's too drenched to tell about. We got to get her out of them clothes and dried off."

"All right."

"Won't she say who she belongs to?"

"Too scared to say anything. Keep that fire coming on."

"Fire's okay. Going like a scalded rabbit. . . . Did I ever tell you that story, Joe Robert, about the scalded rabbits?"

"I don't recall you did," my father said.

And Virgil began the tale of the flatland tourist with his new gold-engraved twelve gauge who went out to hunt him some rabbits and . . . It seemed no fitting time for a windy, my father thought, but then reflected that here were two big rough men who must strip down the little girl and get her warm and save her life and that they must put her at her ease and themselves, too. Even Virgil paid little attention to his story as it went through its quaint convolutions and ridiculous coincidences, laboring toward a supremely silly denouement. It was only a sound he was making, a music for the men to move to as they ministered to the child, peeling her clothes and rubbing her briskly with towels and poking her arms and legs and skinny bottom into a pair of long johns. Then they drew a baggy print dress over her head. It was a curious but effective expedient, and my father added this situation to the list of occasions when mountain people might tell tales. It was wrong, he thought, but it was right, too, nothing could be righter.

They bundled her in a blanket and settled her in a cane-bottom chair by the sizzling stove. She was looking better, rosy now, and her eyes were grateful under drooping lids. That was fine; let her nap in the chair, get a little sleep, it would work wonders.

"Huh-oh," Virgil said. "Where's my tape measure?"

"What's the matter?"

"I don't think this kid'll make the legal size. You're going to have to throw her back in the creek."

He gave Virgil a sad glance. He still looked as miserable as the child had looked, shivering, his clothes clinging wet in some places and dried stiff in others, and the gray serge trousers steaming like a plate of soup.

"We need to get you out of those," Virgil said, "but I ain't got no proper duds here. Just farm work clothes."

"Anything," my father said. "Anything."

They went round the counters and chose a pair of overalls and some cotton underwear and a blue cotton shirt. His shoes would be okay, my father insisted; they had begun to dry out. But after he put on a pair of thick white socks, he discovered that the shoes were too stiff and crusty to get his feet into. He had to pull on a pair of new brogans of the cornball old-fashioned sort; about as pliable as brick, they made a painful fit. It darkened his spirits considerably to understand that his feet would hurt all day long. Bring on your dentist and your Inquisition torturer, he could face them down. But not tight shoes.

He was almost dry now, and that meant worlds to him. He stood by the stove, soaking the heat into his overalled thighs. "So tell me, Virgil, how do I look?"

The sharp baggy little man appraised him slowly top to bottom and back again. "You look like you been to a wedding party and didn't make friends with your new in-laws."

"That bad, huh?" He pirouetted like a high school girl in front of a mirror. His ill-fitting clothes were so starchy

new they seemed to squeak; his creek-smelly hair was
shagged out in thick spikes; the left side of his face was
as lumpy and purple as a blackberry cobbler.

"How'd you get so whupped up? You look like you
been in a cat fight."

"No no, nothing like that," my father said hastily, taking not the least pride in his cat fight. "Just a little accident. Ran into the barn door."

"Three dozen times?"

"Listen, Virgil," he said, "I'm in kind of a pinch.
There's some people going to try to take my job away
from me today. They don't seem to like the way I teach
school and they're going to get on to me about it.
I need to mind my manners and looks my best. It's
plain enough I don't look my best, but do I look so
awful they will just fire me on the spot and be done
with it?"

"Tell them what happened. Tell em you had to jump
in the creek and save this kid's life."

They looked then at the child curled in the chair with
the blanket like a gray squirrel in his nest with his tail all
around him. She slept easily.

"I've run out of time," my father said. "I've got to go
on to school. I'm going to be tardy as it is. You reckon
you can find out who she is?"

"Everybody comes by my store. I know every blessed
thing that happens in this county."

"All right. If anybody needs to get in touch with me,
I'm at the schoolhouse. You'll have to put these nice new
clothes on my bill. But if I lose my job, it'll be a while
before you get your money."

"Don't worry about it. Maybe you'll take up prize-
fighting, what with all your experience."

"Not me," he said. "All I ever want in this world is
peace and quiet."

He hobbled in his angry new clothes out the front door and climbed, aching, into the truck. Started the motor and turned the truck around to cross the little bridge and follow the river upstream to his school, ready to begin this bright Friday all over again for the third time.

Going to be all right, he thought. Third time's a charm.

Three

MEDAL

OF HONOR

In these years, my father did not yet own a watch and now did not know the hour, but he knew he was tardy. The faculty parking lot was already packed with carefully maintained prewar models—teachers couldn't afford the new cars—and rattlebang farm pickups, and the doors to the antiquated three-story brick school-house were shut. When he climbed out of the truck, he fancied he could feel on his skin the silken hum of routine, the murmur of books and blackboards. Not a good day for him to be late, but at least his first class was a study hall. They'd have sent a senior student to cover that one.

He opened the glove compartment and took out his tin of Prince Albert, a book of cigarette papers, and a penny box of wooden matches, and distributed his smoking materials in his overalls pockets. Then he climbed out of the truck and walked across the parking lot.

He mounted the cement steps, opened the door, walked down the hall toward his classroom. Not that it felt like walking, pegging along jerkily as the stiff new overalls cut into his crotch, as the steely brogans burned his feet.

Now don't start whining, he thought. You've got a far way to go today.

Through the panes of the door, he saw Janie Forbes at his desk, monitoring the room with a gaze prim and severe. At their desks, the other students were busy at looking busy. When she spied him standing there, her face registered dismay and she rushed out to greet him.

"Mr. Kirkman," she said, "Mr. Pobble sent me to watch your class."

"*Good* morning, Janie," my father said. "You get prettier every day."

She was a good girl; she blushed and looked down at her clunky saddle oxfords and her rolled white socks. "Oh, Mr. Kirkman."

"When are you going to get rid of that ugly fullback boyfriend so you and I can make some time?"

"You don't have any time," she said. "Mr. Pobble said for you to go to his office."

"Report to the principal's office? What kind of tales have you been telling about me?"

She gave him a straight look. "It's bad enough I don't have to tell any tales. Oh, Mr. Kirkman, we were hoping you'd dress up nice. Everybody knows your job is on the line today. We were just hoping."

"You were hoping I'd find some way to deceive them. Isn't that what you mean?"

A firm declaration: "You couldn't deceive a simple soul."

"Then there's no need to worry, is there? Are the students giving you any sass?"

"Not a bit. We're on your side. We're all going to be lambie-pies."

"Why can't you be lambie-pies every day?"

"I don't know," she said, "but I sure do wish you'd dressed up different."

"Hey-now," he said, "this is the coming style. A little while, and this is what everyone will be wearing."

"Not me," she said.

"Thank you for taking care of my study hall," he said. "Maybe I *had* better run along." But before he left, he rapped on the glass and when the students looked up, he shook his finger at them in half-serious admonition.

He went down the gloomy hall and round the corner toward the principal's office, thinking that Janie was a fine decent girl who couldn't hide her feelings—which meant that he presented an even more shocking spectacle than he'd imagined. Well, no help for that.

He hoped that this new business, whatever it was, wouldn't take long. He'd been counting on an opportunity to collect his thoughts before the afternoon interview with the school board. If it wasn't serious, Pobble wouldn't delay him; he wasn't a bad sort, only rather unbending and officious, the type of acting principal intent on giving an impression of importance. That would count against him when he came to be considered for the permanent position.

Last year, my father had been acting principal and

now he wasn't. His performance, as he recognized, had
not been stellar.

Yet, if only he hadn't gotten caught, he might have
made a life of it. When Jake Silverside died and the job
fell to my father, he'd sat down and thought about this
job, about his duties and responsibilities. He thought for
a solid hour. There was a streak of the philosopher in
him—of William James, perhaps, or Harpo Marx—
which might emerge at the most inappropriate times. As
when, for example, he was tumbling out of a tall poplar
tree with a dandy chance of breaking his neck. And so,
thinking at his desk about the job of being a principal, he
came up with a plan that guaranteed his ruin.

He had long ago noted that one of the most difficult
tasks for a principal was to keep the teachers in order.
They became too ingrown, too concerned with personal
status among equal colleagues, too industrious at gossip,
rumormongering, backbiting, social climbing, petty jeal-
ousy, pointless intrigue, and underhanded politicking.
They were suspicious and envious, and deadly quick to
take umbrage and to imagine injury. They were good
folks—never any doubt of that—but the profession
seemed to work upon them in unwholesome ways. My
father's theory was that once the teachers were led to
become well-behaved, the deportment of the students
would improve.

And so he decided that the teachers needed to be kept
busy; they needed a common cause to weld them into
brotherhood. He invented then the figure of the Ungodly
Terror, a mysterious and utterly rotten kid, a student
who was a danger to them all. He breathed the breath of
life into his myth during his second day on the job. Calling a brief informal meeting of the teachers, he plopped a
shoe box on the chair in front of him, opened it and

produced a quite lively garter snake. The female teachers especially muttered and recoiled.

"Look here now," he said. He held the harmless creature aloft like Perseus brandishing the head of the Medusa. "Look here now, on my very first day as your new principal, I open my desk drawer and what do I find? My very first day. *We've got real trouble here.*" . . . And so on and so on in the hortatory moralizing vein.

It was the Ungodly Terror at work. The longer he went unmasked and unpunished, the greater the risk that all discipline would break down, authority derided and trampled, the whole school collapsing into chaos. "You must have read in the newspapers about New York City and all their problems with Juvenile Delinquency. We don't want that happening here, do we? No we don't." He charged them to search out who the culprit was. "Keep your eyes peeled. Report to me anything that seems out of line. This is our top priority."

He dismissed the meeting then, knowing that they were wary but not entirely convinced.

But that was the best part of the plan, and with wild joy he set about supplying evidence in plenty. He made room in his daily routine to explode firecrackers in lockers, to paint doorknobs with kerosene, to jerk open classroom doors and, hidden from sight by the jambs, fling in handfuls of ball bearings. He filled the teachers' desk drawers with wet oatmeal and their rest rooms with toads. He chalked insulting messages on any wall; not even Kilroy could have matched his omnipresence. In short, he was relentless in carrying out every naughty schoolboy fantasy he could remember.

It must have been for him the Earthly Paradise.

But then there came the morning when one of the older faculty women found him on his knees in the hall-

way, trying to coax a recalcitrant mouse into the ladies'
rest room. It was Rena Preddy, gray and severe in appearance but easy and wryly humorous in temperament.
She was one of his colleagues whom he truly admired,
and he had sometimes thought, If anybody catches me
at these dumb pranks, I hope to God it won't be Rena
Preddy. Yet it was she, and she snatched him by his earlobe like a wayward seventh grader and pulled him to
his feet.

"Do you think the school board will vote me a bonus,
Joe Robert?" she asked. "I seem to have captured the
Ungodly Terror."

At the succeeding conclave, my father made a valiant
and eloquent defense which met with a silence like unto
that of interstellar space. They didn't mind so much what
he'd done; after all, he'd shown himself more a fool than
any of them. But he had damaged the dignity of the profession. What were they to say to the parents who in-
quired about how Joe Robert performed as a principal?

"Oh, Mr. Kirkman is a good man when he's not sprinkling sneezing powder in the blackboard erasers."

They told him plainly that his first term was his last,
that they impatiently anticipated the happy hour of his
removal, and that he shed no glory upon the ideals of
public education.

Well, he thought, I never wanted to be a principal in
the first place.

In fact, he didn't much care for teaching school.
Teaching was my mother's job, but she was still suffering
the effects of a car accident and it was up to my father to
bring in at least a little cash money. He did not fancy
himself as a schoolmarm, but as a farmer, a scientist, an
inventor, an explorer. Look here, he was a wizard just
about ready to come into his full powers. He had been
thinking at length lately of going into the retail furniture

business. In the postwar boom, people had money to spend. Schoolteachers didn't, of course, but real people did. He'd take a few years in business and make his pile, then travel round the world. See what it was that Michelangelo had actually done, see Hoover Dam and the Eiffel Tower, see the architectural wonders built by Izambard Kingdom Brunel.

He was only doing it for the money—but the problem was always money. Money money money. How, for example, was he to pay his debt to the Crazy Creek Wildlife Appreciation Committee? Even after he'd spotted his first fox of the year, he'd still be five hundred dollars behind.

Entering Pobble's office, he suffered a sense of dislocation. Last year this room had been wholly his domain, where he had sat in state, monarch of all he surveyed: budget outlines, requisition forms, attendance reports, grade reports, intercepted mash notes, conference minutes, telephone requests. Of course, he was glad to be out of all that. Of course.

He couldn't imagine why he'd been sent for, but he did feel a bit like a student screwing his courage to the sticking point to face the august powers above.

But that was silly. Here was Dot Whateley, faithful behind her desk, as she had been for nearly twenty years. My father admired her as a kindly woman with a real understanding of pupils, teachers, and administrators. He'd had a little difficulty in asking her to perform her ordinary tasks—it was too much like ordering his mother-in-law about—but she had eased him along. She had, she testified, twelve grandchildren who added daily to her store of understanding and easy authority.

"Morning, Dot," my father said.

She looked him over top to bottom. "Joe Robert, that

is some kind of wardrobe you've got on. Do you mean to signify a particular message?"

"Just pure good taste," he said.

"I'm afraid it's not my style."

"How's Don treating you? Ever I hear he's not treating you right, I'll come in here and kick his heinie for him."

"I don't know that I'd bet on that," she said. "You look like you've been on the losing end."

"Not really," he said. "You ought to've seen what I did to that wildcat."

"I shudder to think."

"Now that you've told me you don't like my looks, was there anything else you called me in for?"

Her face troubled then and her voice darkened. "Don called you in," she said. "This is something different. You remember the Dorsons, don't you?"

"Dorsons?"

"Lewis Dorson's daddy and mama."

"Sure I do." He remembered it all.

"They wanted to talk to you. Something's happened to Lewis, I think."

"Oh Lord. What?"

"I didn't get the whole story. You're the one they wanted to talk to. You're the only teacher they wanted to see."

"In that case, I'd better go in. Thank you, Dot."

He knocked at the door, waited, and entered.

Don Pobble had reddish-blond hair and pale blue eyes. Physically slight, he was a smooth cool customer. Now, for example, he took in my father's wild appearance with a single slow vertical glance but displayed no reaction at all. He rose lightly from the swivel chair behind his desk. "Good morning, Joe Robert," he said. "I'm sure you remember the Dorsons, Pruitt and Ginny."

"It's good to see you again," my father said, gravely shaking hands with Pruitt and nodding to his wife. "How are you-all getting along?"

They gave no answer, and he had expected none. They were shy and ill at ease here in what they would consider a highly public situation, both of them silent farm folk from the genuine old-time mountain stock. Pruitt tilled a rocky small ancestral farm way up near the head of Bear Creek Cove. He'd fed and clothed a family on those flinty acres, four lanky boys and two girls devout and industrious. Hard to imagine how he'd managed, but they were tough, these folks like many others. Yet the breed was disappearing, my father thought. Even the mountains were beginning to change.

Salt of the earth: That was the common phrase for families like the Dorsons, but my father considered that it was all too common. Soul of the earth, he thought, earth's own earth.

The last time he'd seen them was in a painfully embarrassing situation—at least, it had been embarrassing for them. Their son Lewis had returned a highly decorated war hero. Combat had dealt him a terrible and nearly mortal wound. Field surgery had saved him; countless other surgeries had more or less restored him. But he had changed—haunted, nerve-racked, hollow-eyed. The wound was beneath his shirt, nothing showed—yet didn't that make it more terrible, hidden away? He must still live in pain, but there would be no way to know. He was his parents' son; he would walk in stoic silence.

Yet this occasion had made it his duty to talk about himself. He was to give a public speech before a crowd of relatives and neighbors, acquaintances and strangers. He was part of a bond drive for the War Department.

My father felt the profoundest sympathy, remembering Lewis in his General Science class, where he was quiet almost to the point of utter silence. When called upon to recite, he would drop his head and mutter inaudibly, his face blotchy scarlet. He was a good student, nevertheless, interested if not nicely curious, following the discussions with unaltering attention. Never as close with him as with some other students, my father still felt a bond with Lewis; he admired his seriousness and gentle comportment; he admired his willingness.

Just the sort of young man you could never imagine as a war hero. Too easy to think of Lewis as a solitary figure in the woods and fields, happier apart from people, happy with his black and tan hound dog and the colorful seasons. It was the mountaineer strain in his blood, as pure in Lewis as it might have been a century ago.

The effort to sell war bonds brought about the Lewis Dorson Day in Tipton. There must have been hundreds of similar affairs across the country, local heroes doing their part once more. But there must have been very few young men for whom the occasion was so excruciating. Lewis would have faced the enemy artillery with a cooler equanimity.

They erected a platform on the softball field in the middle of town, tacked bunting around it and draped it with flags. From a more fortunate high school in the next county, they borrowed a marching band, and Tipton supplied its own majorettes. The *Herald* gave over its entire front page to Lewis, five separate stories and four photographs, including a picture of the Dorson homestead. There was the little weathered tin-roof shack perched against a scrubby ridge, a tilted well housing on one side and a woodshed on the other. Dim in the grainy background was the gray outline of the outhouse.

Pruitt and Ginny refused to speak but did at last agree

to sit with the other dignitaries on the platform and to rise when introduced. The Baptist minister of their family church kicked it off with a prayer as fierce as a tiger and as long as a railroad. Lewis had chosen my father as his favorite teacher, so it fell to Joe Robert to say that Lewis was a good boy and a fine student. That wasn't quite exact, so he said that Lewis was a fine boy and a good student. Then the mayor—whom my father couldn't abide—had told the stories of Lewis's bravery in combat. We knew these stories by heart, but we heard them again with proud satisfaction. The expression on Lewis's face suggested that he didn't credit a word of this account.

Then it was his turn to speak and he met the occasion. He rose and walked, keeping his eyes fixed on the raw pine flooring until he reached the safety of the lectern. His face blaze-red, he said the words on the pages the War Department had supplied him. His voice was audible though unsteady, the enunciation precise. He delivered the official platitudes with the manner of someone placing coins in a church collection plate.

My father remembered it as Lewis's finest hour.

When it was over, Lewis shook hands with all the people on the platform, even—blindly—his mother, and the band played and a crowd gathered at the booth at third base to invest in war bonds and they seemed glad to do so.

That was the last time my father had seen Pruitt and Ginny, a year ago, and they had hardly changed. Maybe Pruitt was leaner, had weathered a little grayer; maybe Ginny had put on a few gentle pounds. The only other difference was the air of dark sorrow about them. Their quietness had hardened.

They all sat in the narrow straight chairs and Don Pobble spoke to my father. "We have some bad news, Joe Robert. Lewis is dead."

"Oh Lord." But he had known as much. What else could have brought Pruitt and Ginny to the school, to such a public place? "That's an awful thing to hear," my father said. "When did it happen?"

"It was last week," the principal said.

Pruitt spoke. "It was in Detroit city, where Lewis was working there to make cars." His hill twang was as distinct in the office as mandolin notes. "We didn't know nothing about it till last Sunday and we went up there and they buried him on Wednesday. They had doctors going over his dead body, I don't know why. And then we couldn't bring him back home."

"He's buried in Detroit?" my father asked.

"He's buried up there in the biggest graveyard you could think of. A multitude of stranger graves."

That was hard, too, because they would want him in their little Baptist churchyard or maybe in a family plot on one of the back hilltops ringing with bird song, flecked with wild flowers.

"How did it happen?"

Lewis' mother stopped looking into my father's face now. Her mouth thinned to a line like a razor cut and her hands clenched in her lap. She would not break over into full grief, but her iron determination made her look alien and painful in her blue flower-print dress.

"He was shot with a pistol," Pruitt said. "That's all they'd ever tell us. The policemen wouldn't say no more than that. Nobody up there knowed Lewis. He was killed and nobody didn't know nothing, nobody didn't care. He was just a stranger in a strange place, and then he was dead there."

"It's terrible to hear about," my father said. "I didn't even know he'd moved to Detroit."

"He said he went up there to find him a job. But it wasn't no job. He didn't need no money, what with the disability they paid. He was just all restless; he couldn't find no peace after he come back. Get in the truck and ride the roads all day and night and then when he was home, he'd walk the porch boards up and down till sunup. Sometimes he'd sleep a little when it was starting to get light."

"We'll never know how bad he felt," my father said.

"He couldn't have no peace of mind. He left it all over in them foreign lands. We don't believe he ever come back to us, Ginny and me."

"You got to see him, though. So many of them who died over there we never got to see again."

"No." Pruitt spoke sharply. "It was just the same. It was just the same as we never saw him again. We couldn't hardly say who he was."

"I've heard about that," my father said. "There must be a lot of soldiers who came back that way."

"We hope not. We prayed there wouldn't be mothers and daddies that had to go through where we been through."

"Yes," my father said, but he was thinking of Johnson Gibbs, who might have been his brother or even his son and was buried now in our own family plot in Cherry Hill Cemetery and how it was not the least comfort merely to know where he lay after he was killed in the training accident in the army and shipped back in a box and how the telegram that told us about it wouldn't stop plaguing until we were all of us crazy with visions and sorrow. The more he tried to think about Lewis, the more he thought about Johnson and thought of all the good times past and gone and how the world still went on, a world that Johnson could know nothing about.

But he knows about it, Johnson knows. He stands beside us even now as I tell you our story.

"We felt obliged to you," Pruitt said. "At first we was only going to send word. Then we talked about it and thought to come here."

"Obliged to me?" my father asked.

Pruitt drew a worn bulky leather shell pouch from his jacket pocket and set it on his bony knee, let it balance there without touching it with his hand. "Lewis thought a lot of you," he said. "He thought you were a good kind of man. And he got tickled how you would tomfool around. He used to make us grin at the supper table, telling on you."

"I see," my father said, but he didn't. He could not imagine Lewis laughing or grinning.

"We wasn't too sure what to think about that. We never had much schooling, Ginny and me, and we thought the schoolmaster might ought to be more serious. But it tickled Lewis about you, and he was a good boy, and maybe it was all right."

"Joe Robert has a notorious sense of humor," Don Pobble said.

My father gave the principal a warning glance, but Pruitt took no notice. "I can't hardly read at all," he said. "I can read in the Bible right enough, but if it's another book, I can't make much headway. I used to watch how Lewis would pleasure in books that I couldn't make nothing of." He picked up the shell pouch, then replaced it on his knee.

"Lewis was a good student," my father said.

"I don't know if all so many books is a great good thing. I done all right, and my daddy before me and his daddy, with only the Bible. Now we got all the books and the world ain't no better for it, and worse, if anything. But it made Lewis proud to know the books."

"We have to read the books now," my father said. "We'd better find out what they're saying about us."

The gray farmer suddenly leaned forward so far it seemed he might topple from his chair. My father could smell the odors on him now, the salt smell of flannel underwear and lye-washed denim, the sweet smell of cow and leaf mulch and sun-drenched fields. Pruitt peered up into my father's eyes as if he was searching out something in a treetop. Then Ginny touched him on his right shoulder and he sat up straight.

It was the pain then, my father thought, that grabbed Pruitt by the backbone and doubled him over. It'll be a miracle if that pain doesn't kill him within the year. Then he realized that it wouldn't. Pruitt would live with it. It would be with him on the hill at noon and with him in his kitchen at midnight, but it wouldn't kill him.

"I hear tell you lost a boy in the war."

"Not my son, no," my father said. "Somebody close to us. Part of the family."

He nodded as if satisfied, as if my father had passed a test. His agony must have abated now a little, for he picked up the shell pouch again and thumbed the latch open. The leather was dark and glossy and ancient. He held it out to my father, then changed his mind and dumped the contents on the corner of Pobble's desk. It was a tangle of color, a double handful of shiny smudged ribbon and spotted brass. "They gave him all these," he said, "these here medals to be proud of."

"Well," my father said, "they *are* something to be proud of."

Now Mrs. Dorson stood. "Excuse me," she said. "I need to go to the ladies' room." But it was clear that she had planned to quit the scene at this point, and clear, too, that she hadn't told her husband what she was going to do.

He looked at her in surprise. "Wait a minute," he said.

"Not now," she said.

My father opened the door for her. "It's right down the hall," he said. "You ask Dot here. She'll be glad to show you."

"I thank you," she said and squeezed by him and went out. He closed the door gently behind her.

"I hadn't thought," Pruitt said. "She's a strong woman, but it's too hard for her."

"Will she be okay?" my father asked.

"Yes," he said. "She just don't want to be in here right now; she don't want nobody around her. But we decided on this thing together. I reckon it was mainly her idea."

"What had you decided?" Mr. Pobble asked.

He gathered a handful of the medals and held them out. "We wanted Mr. Kirkman here to have one of these if he'd a mind to. To remember Lewis by."

"I don't know," my father said. "That doesn't seem right."

"Ain't they ourn now? Can't we do with them how we want?"

"Yes. But medals are earned. The man who gets a medal has done something to deserve it. I've never even been in the service."

"We got to go by what we believe Lewis would want. We can't think of no other way to do."

"I don't feel worthy," my father said. "It's more honor than I can deserve."

"I can't say as Lewis took so much pride in them. He

stuck them in a shoe box under the bed and that's where
they stayed till yesterday. We took the box out and put it
on the kitchen table and talked about it after supper. It
come to us he'd want you to have something, like one of
these."

"Oh Lord, Pruitt."

"And we said maybe you'd want a remembrance."

"I won't be forgetting Lewis."

"Because of the books, what the books was to him,
and you being the schoolmaster."

My father sighed a hard sigh and made himself relax.
He bent over the mass of ribbons and with a quick stubborn twist of his wrist, he dislodged one from the jumble
as if he were plucking a weed from a flower bed. He
stared at it in his blunt fingers, a stiff little rectangle of
green and red silk, striped like a hard candy. He had no
notion what it stood for and hoped he'd never find out.
He held it up for approval and Pruitt nodded, not looking at the medal, not looking at my father.

"We're obliged," he said.

"This means a lot," my father said. "It's hard to talk
about."

"Something to remember by," Pruitt said.

Pobble spoke to Pruitt then and they began to talk of
the other Dorson children while my father stood silent
and ashamed. It was clear that his part in the visit was
over; Pruitt had accomplished his tense necessary mis-
sion. He excused himself then and went out and, not
speaking to Dot as he pushed through the outer room,
entered the hallway and closed the office door behind
him.

He felt blind. The long dim corridor with its sentinel
rows of lockers seemed endless. It was all shadow, and
his footfall raised echoes that enclosed him like a wall.
He thought about the war. He thought he could taste the

newsprint he'd stared at through those years and could hear the clipped sad mutter of the radio. He was trying not to, but he remembered.

From out of these shadows came another shadow and it took a moment for him to recognize Ginny Dorson in this light, but it was she, walking toward him alone in the grayness. "Mr. Kirkman," she said. There was something she must say to him; she had come out to stand in the shadows and talk to him alone. Already he heard the brittle determination in her voice.

"Ginny."

Her head was lowered so that he looked again into the part of her hair, the thin cloven line vulnerable as a wound. She swayed, unsteady. "It was a thing he wouldn't never tell you," she said.

"Something about Lewis?"

"He shot hisself," she said. "Lewis took a pistol and killed hisself."

"Oh God."

"It wasn't you. It wasn't the books or the schooling. I'm satisfied it wasn't you. Pruitt ain't satisfied, but I'm satisfied."

"It was the war."

She nodded.

"It's no different than if he'd died overseas. It was the war."

She made a little noise, not weeping but not words, either.

He knew better than to touch her. She would pull away from his hand, draw into her body like a sick fledgling bird. She had done her duty now in telling him this, almost in the way that Lewis had done his duty in the war. It was over between them forever now, but my father felt the need to say something, knowing there was nothing to say, yet knowing, too, that she would listen. It came out lame and hoarse: "I thought the world of him. More than that."

"More than the world." She looked into his face. "I count on more."

But that wasn't what he meant, whatever he meant. The world was what my father knew, nothing more or less, better or worse. The world was plenty. "We all do," he said.

She stepped aside now to let him pass by. She would go her way back to Pruitt; he could go where he would. The hall shadows smoothed away the sound of her footsteps.

He went down the hall and pushed into the faculty men's rest room and stood at the tall open window there and rolled a Prince Albert cigarette. It was midmorning, a shining blue spring day outside, robins and white butterflies in the patchy schoolyard grass. In the hallway there with the grieving woman, he had had the feeling that the sky must be gathering to rain, but it was as bright as mirrors outdoors.

If he'd been a praying man, he would have prayed that Pruitt Dorson was wrong, that it wasn't the lessons and the books and the teachers that had brought this century to nothing but disaster. But how could you be sure? Every time you looked anywhere, there was the schoolhouse smack in the middle of it with its fool ideas and its silly hopes. Maybe it was not the cure but the disease, maybe it would have been better always to let well enough alone.

He took the medal out of his pocket and looked at it and it seemed smaller now in his hand than before in the office. Tiny, gaudy, flimsy—like something a child might pick up to treasure out of a weedy roadside ditch, a scrap of cellophane or tin foil. He thrust it back into his pants with a helpless angry gesture and already it began to weigh heavy against his thigh, its heft out of all proportion to its size.

Four

GENERAL

SCIENCE

A curious mixed-up day.

Already it was third period, and my father was just now meeting the first of his classes he'd had a chance to get to. This was his favorite, General Science, which under his purview was a murky broth of General seasoned with a light but noticeable sauce of Science.

Perhaps he would rather have taught in a different way. He declared that he would and had complained about the old dilapidated schoolhouse with its creaky stairways and drafty casements and cold sad gymnasium.

He complained bitterly about his science classroom, which could boast of only one laboratory table with a sink and a Bunsen burner and the proper glassware. Here the teacher was to perform his demonstrations and the students were to sit at their desks and observe in awestruck silence. Dr. Electro unveils the universe.

It was, he thought, the dolefullest situation. There in the squeaky seats before him might slouch a budding Maxwell or a hidden Faraday, who would be lost forever to the world merely because this hayseed mountain community entertained such a benighted attitude toward science that it wouldn't afford the students lab equipment.

The nations who walk in darkness, he thought, and then at the same time he thought of a song he used to sing when he worked for Carolina Electric Corporation. It was a rousing oldtime ballad from the early days of electricity, the decades of Samuel F. B. Morse and Ezra Cornell:

> *Brothers, bear the lighting thong*
> *Down the O-hi-o!*
> *Ten thousand miles of line we've strung,*
> *Ten thousand more to go.*

Many a night round the campfire, he'd sung it with Bill Patton and Tate Whitaker and Dick Lipscomb and that towering Cherokee woodsman, Tiny Tom Raincrow, the guide who kept them in the track to plant the poles and string the wire, to illumine the mystery hills and ridges.

The song reminded him so vividly that he could almost smell the wood smoke and the piny darkness and hear the popping flames as he stood here now and looked without seeing at the students before him, awkward and red-faced in their seats, already bored or distracted, but wondering, too, why their teacher was dressed in such a motley costume and why he looked at them with such a blurred expression on his face.

For my father, too, was distracted and undecided. He knew what was uppermost in their minds and he was wondering how to turn the situation to pedagogical advantage. So he thought What-the-hell-why-not and made up his mind to plow into the issue head-on.

He looked at Daniel Gwynn sitting in the middle of the third row, a square-faced swarthy student with dark and fervent eyes. He liked Daniel, and he realized that he would have to maneuver carefully; he didn't want Daniel to feel that he was being picked on, and he mustn't give that impression to the other students. They knew as well as my father did that it was Daniel's parents, the dour and surly Holy Roller Gwynns, who had brought complaint against him to the school board so that he had to endure a hearing this afternoon. That bunch was getting ready, my father thought, to tack his pelt to the barn door and brand it with Scripture verses.

"Daniel Gwynn," he said, "tell us. Is man descended from the monkeys?"

Daniel didn't flinch or mumble—he was a brave boy—but a scarlet blush spread from the V of his plaid cotton shirtfront to the roots of his black hair. "That's what *you* say," he declared. His voice was not belligerent or even truculent, but it held a note of firm dissent, of protective pride. Whatever happened, whatever the other kids said about him, he was his parents' son.

"Very good," my father said. He turned then to that delight of his every school day, pretty Janie Forbes, who always sat in amused attentiveness in the front row. He thought that Janie might very well have the makings of a scholar, and she used to talk about going to college. Lately she had stopped, and he hoped that she had not given up her dream. Those kinds of dreams were scarce in this time and place—especially for the girls. "Is that what I told the class, Janie, that mankind was descended straight from monkeykind?"

She blinked her lucid blue eyes and laid her chubby hand on her closed blue notebook. "No sir," she answered. "You said that man seemed to be trying to evolve into an animal as nice as a monkey, with an embarrassing lack of success." She drummed her fingers on the notebook. "I wrote it down because I thought it was kind of funny."

"You did?" he said, and it was clear that he was pleased. "You thought it was funny?"

"*Kind* of funny," she said.

He made a moue, deflated. "You want to remember, Janie, the advantages of harmless and diplomatic compliments in a world that sustains itself mainly through hypocrisy, not to say duplicity."

"Well, I wouldn't fib to you," she said.

"And why not, I'd like to know?"

"You'd get to where you liked it."

"Oh, I like it already," he said. "I'm addicted to empty compliments and pointless flattery and I enjoy pretending that these vague noises actually have meaning. They do not, of course. But we who are cowards in society court the comfort of these soothing murmurs because they reassure us that we are liked by other people. Yet maybe it's not the finest thing in the world merely to be liked. I'm thinking of a man who often set out to make himself actively disliked. I am thinking of Dr. T. H. Huxley. Who was he? Who can tell us who Huxley was?"

A strapping blond lad raised his hand, grinning proudly. "He was Darwin's Bulldog."

"That's right, Martin. Can you tell us why he was called by that odd cognomen?"

His grin disappeared like a candle flame snuffed out. "No."

"You've got the main fact," my father said, "if you'll remember that he was tagged with that oppugnant sobriquet because he was able and extremely willing to stand up in public debate in defense of the theory of evolution. You will recall that Dr. Darwin led the quiet life of an invalid and shunned public display, so that T. H. Huxley assumed that the defense of these ideas must fall upon his shoulders. You might also want to recall that he was one of those Victorian educators responsible for the installation of science classes in school curricula. It is partly because of Dr. T. H. Huxley that you enjoy the ineffable pleasure of my company in this science class."

Martin frowned. "Why was he so repugnant?"

"Op," my father said, "not re. This afternoon our baseball team meets the Hayesville baseball team in mortal combat. If we're going to whip their heinie, we have to field a mighty oppugnant team. Oppugnant, meaning spoiling for a fight."

"Okay," Martin said. "I got it."

"Very good," my father said. "Now we've noted before that the really grand ideas, the earthshakers, can never be attributed to a single individual. In speaking of the theory of evolution, we've mentioned not only the names of Darwin and Huxley but also those of Charles Lyell, Alfred Wegener, and a heavy long list of others. We have mentioned also—as we always seem to do— Plato, Aristotle, the Bible, and Sir Isaac Newton. But there is one name we have not mentioned and I think that we ought to consider it. It's an odd sort of name, so I'll write it on the board." He turned and searched the

blackboard tray. "I'll write it, that is, when I can find
something to write with. Where is the chalk?"

"You ate it," said Janie Forbes.

"I ate the chalk? When did I do that?"

"Last time in this science class."

"Did I give any reason for this outlandish feat? I must
have been mighty hungry."

"You told us you were showing the difference between
how the ancient Greeks knew things and how the
Hebrews did. You said that the Hebrews thought we had
to experience everything with our five senses. So you experienced the chalk by eating it."

"Very good," he said. "Did I enjoy it?"

"I don't think so," she said. "You made an awful
face."

"Then I must stop eating chalk," he said, "for I agree
with Alcibiades that a beautiful man should never un-
dertake activities that discompose his facial features. Do
you understand what I'm talking about?"

"I sure don't."

"I sure don't, either," he said. "But I was *going* to talk
about something. I wonder what it was. Oh yes, I remember—Tiglath Pileser." He slid open a drawer of the
lab table, took out a fresh stick of chalk, and printed the
name on the board in ungainly capitals. "Tiglath Pileser:
an unusual name to fit an unusual personality. For one
thing, he was the youngest scholar ever to attend Oxford
University in England. Now during this time—we're
speaking of the 1840s—promising scholars often entered
the university in their tender years. To spot in the quad a
lad of fourteen or fifteen wouldn't be too uncommon.
But Tig—that's what they called him, good old Tig—entered at the age of six months. You'll understand that he
was very proud of his cap and gown and wore his tradi-
tional scholarly dress constantly, often not even disrob-

ing before sleep. He was especially fond of wine parties. At one of the parties given in the Botanic Gardens by the British Association, he allowed himself to be hypnotized. Quite the fashionable thing in those days. Unfortunately, hypnotism doesn't mix well with alcohol and poor Tig passed out completely. When he woke, he must still have been a bit off his head, because he further disgraced himself by riding horseback out to the village of Islip and raiding a grocery store there. He gobbled down every sweet in the establishment, every cookie and cake and candy, nearly frightening the poor shopkeeper out of her wits. This escapade was quite unforgivable, of course, and the university authorities had their prodigy locked up in a big iron cage in the London Zoo. And that, alas, was the whole amazing sad career of Tiglath Pileser." He turned and laid the chalk carefully in the tray. "Now— are there any questions?"

A strong show of hands at once.

"Yes, George Ward?"

"How could they lock him in the zoo? Wouldn't his folks get the law on them?"

"Well, after all," my father said, "he *was* a bear."

"Who was a bear?"

"Tiglath Pileser. Did I fail to make it clear that Tiglath Pileser was a bear?"

All through the room, groans of derision and long-suffering.

"No, now wait," my father said. "What I'm telling you is the truth. Gospel. Maybe I left out a detail or two, but those are the flat facts of the case."

"I don't believe it."

"Nevertheless."

"All right, but so what? Even if it is the truth, what's it got to do with anything?"

"Very good," my father said. "I am coming to that.

The story of our unusual bear is what we cunning
schoolteachers call a *memory aid.*" He turned and re-
trieved the chalk and marked another name on the
board beneath the first. "William Buckland. Please say
this name aloud."

Some of them complied.

"Now every time you hear the name *Tiglath Pileser,* I
want you to recall this other name, *William Buckland.*
Will you promise me to do that faithfully until the day
you die? Raise your hands."

They raised their hands.

"Very good. The reason to remember William Buckland is not only that he was the fortunate owner of the
bear but because he faced in his time the same dilemmas
and perplexed feelings in regard to science that you and I
must face today. William Buckland was a brilliant and
learned fellow, an expert in classical languages and ancient history. Quite early in his life, he took orders in the
church and remained a devout clergyman. But his
strongest intellectual interest was in amateur geology.
That's what he liked to study all day and all night. He
loved geology the way I love catfish marmalade. So why,
then, didn't he become a professional geologist? Who'll
tell us that?"

Linda Butterworth suggested that the Reverend Buckland's parents might have opposed such a decision.

"In fact," my father said, "that became a sore point for
later scientists from upper-class families. All that weigh-
ing and measuring, all that puddling about with acids
and sludges—not something for your mama to be proud
of. Might as well be a navvy or a miner, a member of the
laboring class. But for William Buckland the problem
was that there was no such thing yet as a professional
geologist. He himself was the very first one. Oxford Uni-

versity established the position for him. Now what does this mean?"

Linda suggested that mighty few people would know what he was talking about. George suggested that he wouldn't have much competition.

"Very good," my father said, "and entirely true. But it also means that Tiglath Pileser was the world's first geologist's assistant. So remember now: Whenever we hear the name Tiglath Pileser, we also think of—"

"William Buckland," said they one and all.

"And would you like to know something else about William Buckland?"

"No!" The sentiment was unanimous.

"I was just certain that you would," he said. "Well, he was the first man to name and describe a dinosaur. Megalosaurus, he called it, and it was some kind of big lizard. Looking at the bones and pieces of bones he found, he judged it to be forty foot long and as big around as an elephant seven foot high. He was the first man to imagine that such a monster actually lived upon the earth. There he was, looking at the bones and thinking they must have supported a lizard twice as big as this room. And where do you think he found these bones?"

"In his backyard," George said, "where his dog buried them."

"Never a bit of it. William Buckland didn't even own a dog. He owned a hyena, which would lurk under the sofa and chew the trousers of gentlemen invited to tea. No, I'll tell you where he found those bones. He found them right there in the museum at Oxford, where they'd been on display for Lord knows how long. Think of all the people who looked at those bones and said, 'Gee whiz, these here bones are kind of big.' Or maybe they said, 'Boy-I-declare, them folks back a long time ago raised them some sizable chickens.'

"Then comes along the Reverend William Buckland. He looks at the bones. He walks up and down and thinks. He looks at the bones some more. Sits down and thinks. Looks. Thinks. Then finally he stands up and dusts off the knees of his pants and takes a sniff of his boutonniere and sends up a little silent prayer that he won't go astray and says right out loud the first time without a mistake: 'Megalosaurus.'

"And that's how you get to be a scientific genius. You look at what's right in front of your nose. You think about what you are looking at. Then before you know it, out pops a lizard as big as a barn and as long as a coastline. Bless my ears and whiskers, what a critter it must have been! What a juggernaut! . . . So what did William Buckland decide that this enormous monster ate?"

"Hot dogs."

"Chowchow."

"Ice cream."

"Tiglath Pileser."

"It sorrows me to have to impart this information to you," my father said. "But the natural diet of the Megalosaurus consisted exclusively of the smart-aleck students who populate General Science classes. Which leads us to another problem. The food of the Megalosaurus is, as we can see, still quite plentiful. So why don't we observe these monsters roaring up and down our highways and byways? Why aren't they around in 1946 to instill some good manners in certain bratty young people whom I could name by name if I'd a mind to?

"William Buckland thought again. And came to a conclusion. What was it? What happened to his big lizards?"

Stonky Mewshaw suggested that they went to Holly-
wood to work in monster movies.

"Surely not all of them," he said. "Only the more
photogenic. I think that Daniel Gwynn may help us with
this question. What happened, Daniel, to the dinosaurs?"

He responded firmly. "They drowned in Noah's
flood."

"That's it. That is precisely what William Buckland decided. We mustn't forget that he was a reverend, a sweet
religious man. His big old lizard provided, he said, the
strongest evidence of a universal deluge, proving that
Moses was telling nothing but the truth when he wrote
the book of Genesis. Let us count these firsts for William
Buckland. He was the first man to name and describe a
dinosaur; he was the world's first geologist with the first
geologist's assistant whose name was—"

"Tiglath Pileser!"

"Very good. And he was the first to found a theoretical
school of geology. It was called *diluvial* geology, from the
Latin word *diluvium*, meaning flood, and for quite a long
time it was the single-most-important geological theory.
So there can be no doubt what a great man William
Buckland was. But then, much later on, he did something I think is even more remarkable than anything
he'd ever done before. Would you like to hear what he
did?"

"No no no!" they cried. "Never mention him again!
May his name be blotted forever from the annals of human history."

"I was just certain that you would," my father said,
"because he was not only a great scientist and a jolly fine
fellow, he was also a happy family man, a father who
was careful to educate his own children. He taught them
all about the dinosaurs.

"Now he was often visited by unscientific folk, people who never had the advantage of a wonderful class like ours. They would find old bones and bring them to him to identify. When you become a famous poet, Julia Burnette, all sorts of people will bring you their poems to inspect. When you, Donald Warren, become a famous undertaker like your daddy, people will come to you with different corpses they find lying around. So one day when a fellow minister from Devonshire showed up at the Buckland household with a handful of bones, the good doctor turned to his son and asked him to identify them. 'They are the vertebrae of an ichthyosaurus,' Frankie said. The lad was then but five years old.

"Who will tell us about the ichthyosaurus?"

Not a single solitary soul.

"Mesozoic period," my father said. "Could get up to about thirty foot long. Looked something like a porpoise but with a snout full of dreadful ferocious teeth. Left remains everywhere; ichthyosaurus fossils are very common. But this is the sort of creature that calls into question the whole theory of diluvial geology. What is diluvial geology?"

"Based on the idea of Noah's flood," Janie Forbes answered.

"Very good. Who founded the theory of diluvial geology?"

Some said that William Buckland was the guilty party, others declared that it was Tiglath Pileser, and Rudy Wall identified a wiseass little kid named Frankie.

"Very good," he said. "I'll write it on the board so we don't forget." He turned and wrote beside Buckland's printed name the words *diluvialist extraordinaire*, but his scribble was so illegible it might have been Farsi. "Ah, the dear old ichthyo. He never got aboard Noah's Ark. He was a fish. Noah didn't need to save the fishes from drowning. Forty days and nights of rain are nothing to a fish. But here are all these fossil remains of fish that no longer exist. So, Daniel Gwynn, what happened to them?"

"They died," Daniel said. "Animals die off all the time. They all get sick from something, or there's a big change in the weather."

"Or people kill them off," my father said. "Very good, Daniel. And Dr. William Buckland thought about these causes you have mentioned. He considered them carefully, and he cogitated deeply on other matters, too. And then he did what I admire as being so remarkable. Shall I tell you what Dr. Buckland did?"

"Oh, please please please do!" they cried. "If you ever stop talking about him, our callow young minds will be blighted and impoverished."

"What he did next was to doubt his own diluvial theory. He didn't defend it foolishly in the face of contrary evidence. He didn't turn his back upon it and forswear his theory or the Bible. And he kept on studying geology and writing and thinking, admitting that he was uncertain about the value of his own theories as well as those of other scholars. So what do you think? Isn't that one of the most magnificent feats of pure intelligence you ever heard of?"

"No!" they shouted. "Yes!"

"So tell me, Alvin Smathers. Did you ever hear me say that man was descended from monkeys?"

"You said no human beings were descended from monkeys. Only politicians."

"Herman Caswell?"

"You said the only way I could descend from a monkey was if one kicked me out of a tree."

"Very good," my father said. "There seems to be a wide disagreement about what I actually said. Perhaps

the issue is to remain in doubt. Let us return to the beginning. Daniel Gwynn, what sterling opinion do I hold
about this hotly debated topic?"

Daniel didn't blush or fidget. The effort to remember
showed plainly in his face, but he remained calm and
easy. "I don't know," he said. "I thought I knew, but
now I don't."

"Very good *indeed*. Just like the great pioneer scientist,
William Buckland—and like other genuine scientists in
all ages and nations. The conclusion you have reached is
always irreproachable, Daniel, so long as it proceeds
from honest doubt. If you were bullied into denying a
personal conviction, that would be a different and a dev-
ilish bad thing. Perhaps we can take up the case of
Galileo next class period."

"I just don't remember all that good," Daniel replied.
"Too many people said too many different things."

"We'd better get ourselves together," my father said.
"This hour is just about over. Let's have the boys on the
left-hand side and the girls on the right."

They rose and lined up along their appointed walls,
boys and girls facing each other across the room, the
empty desks between them.

"Boys first," he said.

To the tune of "Cripple Creek" they sang—con brio:

> *"Named for the great Assyrian king,*
> *Tiglath Pileser could dance and sing."*

"Girls," my father said.

They sang:

> *"If he got drunk on wine, who cares?*
> *He was the best of all the bears."*

"Now all together."

> *"All hail to William Buckland! He*
> *First invented geology,*
> *And showed us, in this world below,*
> *We don't know all we claim to know."*

"Very good," my father said. "All hands left and do-si-do."

Five

THE

REHEARSAL

Sanford Slater and my father were old friends. They had met before Joe Robert Kirkman was my father, before he married Cora Sorrells, sixteen years ago, a year before time began. This meeting took place during my father's first stint as a schoolteacher, when he had first arrived in the mountains from the eastern middle part of the state. He had prepared himself to teach school but then had discovered the job too tame for him, too limiting. He tried a number of professions and wound up a farmer, a dreamer, and a carefree scapegrace. But for him these occupations were only stopgaps. For the present time he was forced to teach school once more, but his glory days were coming. He could feel the bright glow of them on his face like a rising dawn.

Sandy and Joe Robert became cronies, hunting and fishing together at all opportunity and trading scandalous jokes about the other teachers. They had both endured separate year-long terms as basketball coach and had achieved equally disastrous records. They shared an exasperation with the local politics and with the dependence of the welfare of the school upon political patronage. Hiding some of their darker feelings with humor, they sometimes discussed the shortcomings of the teaching profession in this remote and skeptical community.

The truth of it was that Sandy Slater and my father would have preferred to board up the classrooms and to traipse with students through field and grove, by road and stream, pointing out oak galls and muskrat dens and bee trees and deer sign, naming this weed and that wild flower in both common and Linnaean nomenclature. These two men agreed upon a priority of delight.

So when my father ran afoul of the Gwynns, the unhappily religious parents of one of his brave students, and when it became common knowledge that he must face an inquiry by the school board to determine whether he might keep his job, Sandy wanted to come to his aid. There seemed little that he could do, since the course of events was fixed. The preliminary hearing was to be held on this Friday at two o'clock in an empty classroom. If worse came to worst and there was a public hearing, then Sandy could appear as a character witness and tell every interested party that my father was a gentleman and a scholar, and rather a humorous sort of fellow, and just about the most thoroughly practiced liar a man could ever hope to meet. Or he could tell some lies himself if they would benefit Joe Robert and if he could keep a straight face while reeling them off. "Just as long as I don't have to declare that you're some sort of basketball genius," Sandy said.

"You won one game and lost eleven," my father replied. "Do you really imagine that they're going to call on your basketball expertise? Anyhow, I don't aim for it to get to a public hearing. I'm going to head them off at the pass, at the preliminary."

"How will you do that?"

"I don't know yet."

"Maybe we can figure it out," Sandy said. "We know the board members, we ought to be able to guess the sort of thing each one of them will be looking for. What we'll do, you and me, we'll get together and have a dress rehearsal. You can knock em on their asses."

"It's not a bad idea." My father brushed his earlobe with his thumb knuckle. "When's a good time for you?"

He considered. "The best time," he said at last, "would be during lunch period on the day of the hearing. That way, it would be fresh in your mind and you'd be geared up for it emotionally."

"Gearing down is what I need," my father said. "I want to be able to hold on to my nerves and my temper and my lunch."

"I'll go through the list of board members we're pretty sure will show up and write down the kind of question I figure each of them might ask. You do the same thing. Between us we ought to hit pretty close to the mark. After all, these folks are our neighbors."

My father began to take a quicker interest in the notion. "Sure they are," he said. "This is a kind of *psychological contest*. I bet I can hit it right on the nose, exactly what every last one of them will ask."

"Well now, you don't want to get too cocky."

"How could I miss?" he said.

So now the hour appointed had come round and Sanford Slater and my father avoided the faculty lunch table
and ducked out a north-side door of the building. This
door opened into a dead area of the school grounds, a
large square cinder yard enclosed by the walls of the
building on one side and by a deeply eroded high clay
bank on the other. Two rickety fire escapes, black paint
blistered and peeling, let down into the cinders at op-
posite ends of the yard. It was a forbidding space tucked
away back here, usually avoided by faculty and students
alike. Rats and lizards in there, and maybe snakes.

Sunk beneath the cinders were cement steps leading to
the entrance of the basement boiler room. Sandy went
down first; his stocky figure descending tipped back and
forth like a bell buoy. He shifted his paper lunch bag to
the other hand and fished out his key ring and opened
the Yale lock inset into the green steel-sheeted door. He
pushed it wide, reached blindly for the switch, and
turned the light on. He held the door open for my father.
"Age," he said, "before beauty."

"Myth," my father replied, "before history. Thought
before action." He paused there on the landing to look
into the room.

The wooden stairs led down into a large gloomy room
pungent with dust and lumpy with shadows. The space
at the bottom of the steps was dominated by the big furnace with its dull gray ceramic jacket. An ancient coal
burner, it had recently been converted to oil in one of
the many pointless halfhearted attempts at modernization that periodically plagued the school. "They claim
they want to modernize this place," my father would
say. "The only modernization that would help would be

Hiroshima." There was a fairly new-looking wall of raw
plywood behind the furnace; it cut the room in two on
that side and performed, as far as Joe Robert could make
out, no function whatsoever. One more puzzle. In front
of this plywood wall was stacked or laid or heaped the
usual sort of junk you'd find in an institutional spare
room: boards, sawhorses, empty jugs and mason jars,
yards of canvas, broken window frames, stacked panes
of glass, rolled oilcloth, dirty tubes of brown wrapping
paper, half-bales of seagrass twine, and so forth. There
was a mildewed old armchair covered with a filthy
chintz and a wobbly straight chair with a cane bottom
that sagged like a pregnant mare.

My father bounced down the stairs—which vibrated
and rattled threateningly—and flung himself into the
armchair. A fine white bad-smelling powder boiled out
of it and covered his hair and clothes like a dusting of
flour. "Oh shoo," he said. "What the hell is this stuff?"
He stood up and spanked at his overalls with both
hands.

Sandy Slater lowered himself into the balloon-bot-
tomed straight chair with dignified delicacy. "How come
you're always flinging yourself about like a tumbling
act? That chair's full of plaster dust. They left it sitting in
that room back of the auditorium when they tore the
walls out. It has been a prop in many a thrilling senior
play."

"Just look at me," my father said. "I'll never get this
stuff out of my clothes before the hearing."

"No, I don't think you will," Sandy admitted. "On the
other hand, I'm not sure they'll notice that single odd
detail."

"I look pretty hopeless, eh?"

"Just what in the world did you have in mind with
that getup you're wearing? That's going to count so tall

against you that it hardly makes any difference what you say. Of course, this is just a guess on my part. That outfit might be the absolute one that the school board likes best in all the world."

"Sorry," my father said. "But the way it turned out, I didn't have any choice. Maybe if I can get some of this plaster dust out." He slapped his bib and shirt-sleeves and dust exploded from him as if he were the clock of a dandelion blowing off in a puff of wind.

"No no, that's not the problem. Actually, it kind of adds something."

And in fact, this cake frosting of white powder did add something that seemed to have been missing from his costume: a sign of the professional clown, a touch of disconsolate Pierrot, mournful and funny.

Sandy continued. "If I'd known you were going to suit up like some burlesque comic, I'm not sure I'd've given up my lunch hour. And what happened to your face? You look like eight rounds with Joe Louis."

"I had to wrestle a wildcat," my father said. "It came as a surprise."

Sandy gave him a sharp green-eyed glance and said, "I'm not prying into your private life, Joe Robert."

"I don't take it as prying. Because I don't have a secret in the world. What I had, no joke, is a fight with a wildcat. I'm itching to tell you about it when we get the time, but now we want to practice up for this afternoon. I appreciate how you're giving up your lunch hour and I'll pay you back for it. I'll get Cora to bake you one of her rhubarb pies. . . . Or, wait a minute—I'll make you one myself. Do you know, I kind of fancy that mine are just a wee bit better than hers? Don't say I said that and I'll tell you what my secret is. Soak the rhubarb in Cheerwine overnight beforehand. You ever hear of doing that? Cheerwine."

Sandy's tone was grim. "It sounds delectable. And speaking of delectable, where's your lunch bag?"

"I left it upstairs on purpose. Truth is, I'm too nervous about this afternoon to eat." Truth was, he'd forgotten to make his lunch, preoccupied in the early morning with that Normandy invasion of a breakfast meal he'd engineered.

"You sure? I've got plenty here—a ham sandwich, banana, milk. Plenty for both of us."

"I couldn't choke it down if you paid me." He watched with feral fascination as Sandy unstoppered his pint of milk and shucked the wax paper from his sandwich. He was famished, he was ravenous, he could eat every pig the World Almanac had tallied for the year.

"So now, how do you break it down?" Sandy asked.

"Break down what?" my father asked, watching with hypnotic intensity the corner of sandwich that went into Sandy's mouth.

"The school board this afternoon. Which ones do you figure to be on your side?"

He sat carefully on the arm of the dusty chair and leaned forward confidentially. "Here's how I figure it. Four members will show up for certain, and maybe six. For certain we'll have Cale Smathers, Handy Conrad, Irene Macclesfield, and Ben Meaders. Then we'll probably get Jack Coble or Susie Underwood."

"That's my count, too," Sandy said, "except that I'm also expecting Baird McDowell."

"Lord, I hope not."

"How come is that?"

"We had a bit of a run-in one time. Little business of a runaway heifer. Didn't amount to much, but it's the sort of thing he'd remember."

"Okay." Laying the uneaten half of his ham sandwich on his knee, Sandy drew a notebook and gnawed pencil stub out of his shirt pocket. "We'd better make a few notes. Anybody else in this bunch who might harbor hard feelings?"

My father thought. He thought for a good long while, and even after his friend evinced unmistakable signs of impatience, sighs and shiftings and twitches, he thought some more. Finally he said: "Every last one of them."

"You're kidding."

"You know how it is. It's a small community; we've all had dealings with one another that haven't been one-hundred-percent pleasant. If somebody wants to do you a bad turn, he's always got something he can remember. Doesn't have to be much. My boy Jess ran his bike through Susie Underwood's petunia bed. Just an accident, and I think we got it all straightened out. But if she wanted to hold it against me . . ."

"Now this surprises me. I'd've said you're the one man I know with all the friends he'll ever need. It's just that you can't name them in this bunch—is that right?"

"I'm choicy," my father said. "I prefer the company of whittlers, whistlers, and wildcats."

"Who doesn't? But they're not the type of folks that wind up on school boards. And anyhow, none of these members are dead set against you. You pour on your boyish charm and you'll have em eating out of your hand." But he tucked the little notebook and the pencil stub back into his pocket.

"I don't feel as boyish as I used to. I may be maturing. I may be turning into the sort of upright citizen my mother-in-law has hoped for."

"Just be sweet and polite and tell them what they want to hear."

"But what is it they want to hear? That evolutionary theory is a communist plot and Charles Darwin is Satan's instrument on earth?"

Sandy took an earnest swig of milk and set the bottle on the floor. He rested forward in that position with his hands on his knees and looked up into my father's face, all scratched and battered and lumpy and pale with plaster dust. "That's exactly what they want to hear."

"Well, that's exactly what I'm not going to say."

He sighed and nodded and sat up straight. "And they know you too well to expect that you would. So they'll probably ask in general terms about your religion."

"All right."

"Well?"

"Well what?"

"What's your religion?"

"I hold," said my father with grave pride, "the religious principles that every sensible person holds."

"Which are?"

"No sensible person talks publicly about his religion."

"With that attitude, you're dead in the water."

"I've got every right to keep my religion private. It's in the Constitution."

"This crowd," Sandy said, "goes terrible light on the Constitution and terrible heavy on the Bible. So: Have you prayed to Jesus Christ down on your knees as your personal savior about whether you ought to be teaching evolution?"

"I've thought about it hard and at length. My reasoned conclusion is that I ought to teach the classic theory of evolution."

"But you're a public servant," Sandy said, "and you're answerable to the public the same way a senator is, or a dogcatcher. So why should a righteous and upstanding family like the Gwynns pay their hard-earned tax dollars to this representative of the Antichrist, this Joe Robert Kirkman, who teaches their son Daniel just precisely what they don't want him to be taught?"

He didn't hesitate. "They shouldn't. They should keep Daniel at home under lock and key and teach him whatever it is they want him to learn. And they shouldn't pay any public-education taxes."

"That's impossible. The law in this state says that he has to attend public school. If he's not here, they send an officer to fetch him."

"Then it's a bad law," my father said, "and they ought to get rid of it. The way I see this whole problem is that it begins with me. I'm a teacher. That's what I am wherever and whenever I teach. I don't particularly want to be a schoolteacher, but right now I am one. So I have to teach what I think is the truth, whether the state pays my salary or nobody does. Otherwise, I'm *not* a teacher and have no right to receive a salary. If taxpayers want to pay me to teach things I believe to be untrue, they'll have to hire me as an actor, somebody who just reads the lines. But I'm not an actor and I won't take their money to say things I don't believe."

"It's been my observation," Sandy said, "that your most outstanding talent is in leaving the truth a homeless orphan. I'm not going to call you a liar, Joe Robert, but I do have to say that exaggerations, dissimulations, and prevarications seem to seek out your presence and to grow sleek and contented in your company."

"That is a different matter," my father said, "and pretty well covered in Aristotle's *Poetics*, where he speaks of that species of lie that aims to reveal a *general* truth. Now that's the kind of lie I'm telling day to day, hour to hour. Parables, if you will—the kinds of lies Jesus used to tell. But teaching science is a different thing entirely. Science demands factual exactness and mathematical precision. I'm not going to stand in front of a class and say that God made all the various animals in a single week and in His spare time deposited the fossil record so that people would have something to fuss about. That's not a scientifically accurate fact."

"How do you know it's not?"

"God told me it wasn't. He said it was the silliest load of tripe He'd ever heard of."

"Well, maybe you don't need to argue the point. That's as convincing a piece of scientific evidence as I've ever been presented with. Did He also happen to let you know what questions His righteous flock is going to put to you?"

"I think I've about got it doped out on my own. Take Handy Conrad. He's a hardheaded farmer who raises purebred Hereford stock. I think he'll ask me if I believe acquired characteristics can be inherited. That would be in his line of business, you see. And Irene Macclesfield teaches Sunday school, so she'll be interested in Bible history. She's liable to ask me if I believe the geological record favors gradualism or the cataclysmic theory. Why are you looking at me all goggle-eyed?"

Slowly Sandy closed his mouth and blinked his eyes into focus. "You're serious, aren't you?"

"Serious how?"

"I mean, you really think that's the kind of questions they'll ask."

"I think I'm pretty close."

"It's hard to believe, Joe Robert, that you don't have an inkling."

"Sure I do. They want to nail my hide to the barn door. But they've got to do it with proper questioning."

"No they don't and I think you're aware that they don't. I hope you won't take this the wrong way, Joe R., but I get the feeling that what you really want, when it's all over and done with, is the choice between exile and hemlock and that you've already decided to drink the hemlock."

"No," my father said. "Oh no no no." He was vexed and embarrassed. "I don't want Socratic dialogue, I don't want any sort of drama whatsoever. I want to avoid confrontation. What I want to do is keep my job and I am willing to say to them, Excuse me Ma'am and Sir, I meant no harm to God or Jesus or you or anybody else with my brief excursion into accepted biological theory and if you-all will please allow me to kiss your plush-lined and gold-mounted asses I will do so with all alacrity and then we can all say that justice has been meted out. How does that sound? If I was the school board I'd be satisfied with that and more than satisfied."

Sandy unpeeled half his banana and levered it up and down in the traditionally obscene gesture. "They'll be satisfied you're giving them *this*," he said. "I thought you didn't want a fight?"

"I don't."

"Then why do you come charging at them like old Jackson's bull just a-snorting?"

"They piss me off. Look here, these are good folks, none better to be found in the nation. But they've got no right to ask these kinds of questions and they know it. And they know I know. So it's plain dumb and silly on both sides."

"They've got the right." Sandy bit his banana. "As soon as Daniel Gwynn's parents appealed to them, they had the right."

"Well, I'm going to get by them, whatever it takes."

"All right, but it's not easy. If they ask you if evolution is morally wrong and you say no, you've got one foot in a cow pie. Then when they ask you about geological time scale, you've got the other foot in quicksand. Then when they ask you if the Bible is literal and infallible history, you've got your manly butt in a bear trap. I'd

like to be there at that moment to watch the kind of
strategy you pursue."

"You're not being helpful," my father said. "I'm willing to kiss ass, and you say that won't work. I'm willing
to tell innocuous lies, and you say that won't work, either. I'm willing to be open and honest with them up to
the point that it's any of their damn business, and you
say no. What you mean is that nothing I say will do the
least bit of good."

He thought it over. "Maybe it's not so much what you
say as the way you say it. There's a certain tone of voice
you have when this matter comes up that sounds polite
enough on top but underneath is telling people to go
take a flying leap. There's something in your manner
that says that your personal independence is what is
most important to you and the other considerations have
to take a backseat."

"That's not the impression I want to—"

"I admire your spirit and courage and all that, but
then I think, Wait a minute now, Joe Robert's a family
man."

"Indeed I am."

"And I think, If I was in his place, if I had me a lovely
wife and two fine younguns—"

"You'd ease off."

"I'm not sure what I'd do. It's a lucky thing I'm teaching math; we don't get a lot of topical controversy in
algebra class."

"Wait now," my father said. "What about these newfangled theories of number? Don't they cause a little stir?
How about Cantor and Gödel?"

"I save those abstruse debates for my Ph.D. students.
Which have been running pretty scarce here lately."

"But you want your kids to know the issues. You want
them to hear the names, at least."

"I want them to hear the expression *binomial theorem*," Sandy declared. "I want a girl to come into class and sit down and take out her chewing gum and replace it with the words *binomial theorem*."

My father shook his head. "That's not the way you think about teaching."

"Sure it is."

"Since when?"

"Since today. Or yesterday. Or last week."

"How come?"

"Don't you ever get fed up? It wasn't so long ago the state didn't even pay its teachers for a month's work. Maybe I'm tired and fed up."

"Nah."

"Maybe I'd like a little security. Maybe I'd like to put in my time and draw my pension."

"Never."

"Maybe I'm fixing to be a family man myself and it scares me shitless." He dropped the banana peel into the paper bag with the wax paper and empty milk bottle and rolled up the bag and stuck it under his arm.

My father blinked five times. Then he gulped. Then he broke into a grin like a splinter of fatwood catching fire. "Married," he said softly. Then he spoke louder. "Married, by God! Sandy Slater has been *hooked*."

Sandy blushed as red as the rooster's comb. He glanced up at the cobwebby ceiling and then looked attentively at the furnace on his right-hand side and wound up staring fixedly at the plywood wall behind my father's chair.

"Who's the lucky girl? Unlucky, I should say."

"Well, I haven't asked her yet. Maybe she won't have me."

"But you know who she is, don't you?"

"Well yes."

"And would you rather tell me here and now or have your brains dashed out with a two-by-four?"

"Lnn Bn."

"Who?"

"Lnnn Bnn."

"Will you for God's sake speak up?"

"LINETTE BANKS."

"All right," my father said. "Simmer down. It's not good manners to be hollering out the name of your intended. My goodness, Linette Banks. That's our new Home Ec teacher, eh? She's awful pretty."

"She sure is."

"Teaches these girls how to cook and sew and keep house. So she's an expert in that line."

Sandy nodded.

"Oh, you're the sly one. Got the new girl in town and just about the prettiest one in the county and the one that knows where the kitchen is. You're too many for me, you are. When are you going to ask her?"

"Soon," Sandy said. "Just as soon as I can figure out what to say."

"I'll tell you what to say. You say, Linette, my little honeylamb sugardumpling, let's you and me get hitched. Simple as that."

"Is that the way you put it to Cora?"

"Well no, but mine was a special case."

"What do you mean?"

My father paused. "This is another religious problem," he said. "And no sensible man ever tells another man what he said when he proposed to his beloved wife."

"You're no help."

"Oh yes I am. I'll go through it with you step by step. We'll whip it down to a fine polish. She'll say yes before you know what hit you."

"Listen to Mr. Diplomat," Sandy said. "I'm supposed

to take lessons from a man who can't talk well enough to keep his own job?"

"You ought to listen to me because I'm an expert. Been happily married for fifteen years, got me two healthy children and a mother-in-law as sharp as Clarence Darrow."

"So you lucked out."

"Folks get the wrong impression. Everything that happens to me is according to a plan I've been working on for years, a plan audacious in scope yet bold in its simplicity. Everything you see me do is but a necessary stage in the completion of this grand design."

"You mean, greeting the school board looking like a traffic accident dressed up like a circus clown."

"There are bound to be a few hitches. But this will all work out. All I have to do is talk sweet and eat a little humble pie."

"That's what you think now. But what if you have to grovel and lie?"

"A small inconvenience." He flashed Sandy a cheerful grin. "Glad to do it, if it means putting bread on the table, laying by a little nest egg for the family. Now that you're going to be a married man, you'll be thinking along these lines."

"I'll tell you what," Sandy said. "If I hear tell that you knuckled under for the sake of your family, I'm going to think twice about everything."

"The thing to do is to get married. You-all will be so happy this other stuff won't even seem like a problem."

"I'm going to watch and wait," Sandy said. "But not down here in this basement. I've got a class in six minutes."

"Me, too. But you go on ahead. I'll rest here a little bit and try to think through a few answers."

"Want me to feed you some more questions?"

"I'd better just sit and ponder and maybe pray."

"All right." He stood up and offered his hand. My father rose and they shook. "Good luck," Sandy said.

"Thanks."

He climbed the stairs to the exit door, then turned at the top to give a jaunty mock-military salute. "You'll do fine," he said.

"Nothing to it," my father replied.

And when Sandy had gone out and my father sat alone in the junky basement in that malodorous chair full of plaster dust, he thought, Yes indeed, he would do fine and there was nothing to worry about. The more important thing was that Sandy was getting married, and he looked forward to telling my mother about that event the first thing when he got home that evening. She was always complaining that he never brought home news or gossip. That was what she missed most these days, not being ready yet to go back to work. She wanted to know what was happening, what her friends were up to, but my father was useless. Gossip didn't stick; he was too high-minded, or too absentminded, or perhaps merely obtuse on one large side of his nature. At any rate, rumor left no impression upon him. But this was different. Sandy was getting married, and that was real news, fresh and important.

They'd have to give a nice party for Sandy and Linette. And he'd have to begin thinking of some sterling practical jokes to play on them. Your everyday garden-variety prank wouldn't do for a wedding, no sir.

He thought upon these matters and he thought upon others. He was furiously hungry and he was beginning to feel a little tired, but there was still a long way to go this day, and so he got up slowly and slowly climbed the creaky steps to the landing and laid his hand on the cool knob of the exit door.

But then when he clicked off the light, he saw another different light in the floor space below. It was a dimmer light, more orange than yellow, and not pervasive but slicing through the dark room in four thin sheets. It came from the center of the plywood wall behind the dusty armchair.

He waited for his eyes to adjust, then made his way carefully down again, the steps seeming to creak more loudly in this semidarkness. When he reached the bottom, he waded almost blindly toward the wall and the light.

The four lines of light etched a rectangle in the wall and he felt along those edges with his fingertip, along the top and down along the sides. I know what this is, my father thought. There is a secret door in this wall.

He put his eye to the crack on the left-hand side, but the crevice was too small and he could see only more orange light on the other side. Light only, and no detail, no objects.

He puzzled at it for a moment and then began to search for a way to open the secret door and go beyond.

SHARES

My father and Hob Farnum found one point upon which they enjoyed perfect agreement. They both hated and passionately despised the system of tenant farming. My father considered it a degrading cheat. "Hard enough to support one family on a farm these days," he said. "Takes a lot more farm than we've got to support two families. And on top of that, there is supposed to be profit, real cash money profit that the landowner and the tenant split between them. But there never is any profit and when it's time to deal out the shares, the tenant gets nothing. He has to borrow again from the owner. It keeps him poor forever

*and it breaks his pride. Turns him mean sometimes. . . .
Now I'm not talking about Hob when I say that.''*

*But, yes, he was talking about Hob. The situation was
that Hob and his family lived on the farm during the middle war years as tenants. We had no choice, what with my
mother unable to work for three years because of a car accident, and Johnson Gibbs dead now, and my father teaching school to bring in that pittance of money. It didn't
matter what he thought about the tenantry system; he was
stuck with it.*

*Hob Farnum was fierce. A short man, slightly
hunchbacked, he was filled with an angry narrow energy.
Farming on shares was an unjust system, so he was a victim of injustice, and it didn't matter to him what we felt
about it, the irreducible fact was that we owned the land
and he helped to farm it because he owned none, and the
system was not going to change. This was what he'd done
all his life and all his life he had hated it. In his squeezed
red face, his glassy eyes shone like drops of coal oil and
expressed his fretfulness. He was a furious man, he didn't
care who knew it.*

*We were riding, the four of us, in a crude sled. We
scrubbed along over the half-buried rocks and gravel in the
muddy road. There was Hob and his son Burrell and his
daughter Bess and there I was, the grandson of the woman
who owned the farm, my father's son, and living with my
family in the big brick house on the crest of the hill, the
house shaded by tall flame oaks and a walnut tree.*

*Bess was five years old. She sat, with her chubby dirty
legs thrust out from her torn dress, toward the front of the
sled, watching the plugs of mud fly up from beneath
Maud's hooves. Burrell, who was a year older than me,
was tinkering with the plow that lay on the sled. It was a
gray cold day in early spring and though the ground was
too wet to turn, we were transporting the plow to the far*

field, where it would be waiting when the weather cleared.
I was standing behind Hob who only occasionally urged on
the big black mare. "Git on, Maud," he would say and
give the lines a casual fillip.

Burrell was still fooling with the plow, tinkering with
the handle brace. He stepped over the long tongue to get to
the other side and, just as he did, the sled bumped through
a rut and threw him against me. My hand shot out of my
pocket and flicked the shoulder of his worn and peeling
leather jacket. It wasn't a blow; I wouldn't strike him deliberately. I was only blind in some private fantasy and I
pawed out without thinking, the way Maud would switch
her tail at a sweat bee. It was an act unpremeditated, certainly without malice, and Burrell only glanced at me
briefly, showing no emotion, and turned back to the plow.

But Hob had seen. He stopped the sled. "Are you going
to let him put that on you?" He fixed Burrell in a wild
glare.

"Let him put what?" Burrell asked.

"Let him get away with slapping you like that."

"Wadden nothing," Burrell said. "I didn't even feel
it."

"Letting him give you a slap. The back of his hand."

"What do you care? He didn't hit you. What're you
carrying on about it for?"

"Now a man might give me a lick sometime and get
away with it. That would have to depend. But ain't no
man going to slap me, to show how he thinks I'm low."

"Yes, but if I'd've hit him back, you'd lay into me for it.
You done said you would."

"Not for a slap," the gnarled man said. "For a slap,
I'd bless every blow you struck."

"Wait a minute," I said. "I was just pushing him
away, kind of, so he wouldn't fall on me. I didn't mean to
slap him."

He didn't glance at me; I was no more to him now than
a weed in the roadside ditch. He held Burrell steady in his
gaze and said, "You've got my word now I won't whup
you if you want to take him on."

"I don't see what for."

"You ain't scared of him, I reckon."

Burrell reddened. He seemed to choke off a retort before
he turned to me and made his vague offer. "You want to
get down here now and we'll have us a go-round?"

"No," I said. "I didn't mean nothing, it was just an
accident. I'm sorry about it and I apologize." The situation
made no sense to me. Boys have their own ways of settling
things among themselves and when grown-ups interfere, it
all becomes confused.

Hob asked Burrell: "Does that satisfy you, him saying
he's sorry?"

"What do you think? You the one making all the
ruckus."

"It wouldn't satisfy me. Not for a slap."

He was puzzled, but Burrell was happy for the opportunity to punch me around. He stepped off the sled into the
mud and gravel. "All right. Get him to come down offn
there, I'll whup his ass good. As long as you don't whup
mine when I've done it."

"I won't lay a hand on you," Hob said. "I just want to
see you stand up like a man." He turned his wild oily eyes
on me. "You want to get down and get with Burrell? I
warrant you it'll be a fair fight."

"I don't want to fight," I said. "I didn't mean to do
anything to Burrell. There's no use to be fighting."

"He's offering you fair and square."

I shook my head. "No use in it. Burrell's stouter than
me a whole lot. He's proved he can get me down lots of
times."

He asked Burrell, "What's he talking about? Have you been fighting with him before?"

"Play-fighting," Burrell said. "Not like no real fight."

"I don't understand this play-fighting. A man fights or shows hisself a coward. What does he mean by it, play-fighting?"

"Like in the picture shows, the cowboys," Burrell said. "He likes the picture show stuff where we don't really hit, just play like we're hitting."

"I never heard the beat," Hob said. "Big boys like you-all. That would be something you would see Bess doing, playacting."

Bess turned to look at her father when he spoke her name. Her eyes were large in her smudged face and her mouth was open. She had been crooning to herself the soft wordless tunes she was always making.

Burrell seemed more confused than ever. "Well, you told me to keep them happy here, and that's what this 'un likes to do, and so I done it."

"I didn't figure what kind of foolishness it would take. A big boy like you, fifteen years old." He turned to me again and seemed even more irritated than before. "You want to get down from the sled and fight him now? A real fight, all fair and square?"

"I'm not but thirteen," I said. "Burrell's bigger than me and stouter. He'd beat me easy."

He looked at me a long time then, as if I were changing shape before his eyes. "What if he was to name you a yeller coward?"

I shrugged.

"What if he was to say he saw your grandmaw giving titty to a nigger man?"

I felt my neck and ears burn. It embarrassed me to hear him talk. "I didn't hear Burrell say anything like that."

He spoke to Burrell. "Say it."

Burrell sighed a heavy sigh and repeated the words in a dull uninterested tone.

"Now you heard him," Hob said to me. "What're you going to do about it?"

"Nothing," I said. "It's not worth taking a licking for."

He kept looking and looking at me. Finally, he shook his head. "I ain't never seen the beat. A young feller showing hisself a yeller coward like you do. It plumb beats me. It does now."

"I don't like getting beat up. Burrell knows he can do it. What's the use of it?"

"Damn right I can," Burrell said. "I just been itching to whup your ass good."

"Well, he's right about one thing," Hob said. "If he's showed hisself a yeller coward, they ain't no use in whupping him." He clucked at Maud and the sled jerked forward.

Burrell hopped up on the back of the sled as it went past. Trotting forward to keep his balance, he blundered into me, striking me in the chest with his shoulder. I went toppling off the sled, flat on my back in the muddy road.

"Hey," I said. "Watch out."

"What for?" Burrell asked. "What have I got to watch out for?"

There was too much about the situation that I couldn't understand and I couldn't bring myself to talk to my father. He had always told me to avoid fights and had expressly forbidden me to fight with the children of the tenant farmers. The fights themselves were harmless, he said, but there were complex feelings, complex issues that emerged and it would be better if I didn't fight. My father understood things I could never understand, but I knew already that he would not understand the dilemma I was in now. He would see it as petty and trivial and he wouldn't know the dreadful black shame I had brought upon myself.

Once before, when I was ten, I had fought with a tenant boy and had taken a sound thrashing. It was a point of honor with me that I had taken the licking and had not bawled, had not shed a single tear. But when my father heard about the scrap, he was displeased and took me out into the yard under the walnut tree and put his hands on my shoulders and stared hard into my face. "Didn't I tell you not to fight?" he asked.

"Yes," I said, "but I didn't start it. Jerry started it."

"Hush up about starting it."

"Yessir."

"Listen here," he said. "Poor people have got plenty enough problems without you hitting them. Maybe you don't know about these things yet. All you have to know is not to fight with them."

"Yessir, but I didn't—"

"Just don't do it," he said. "Just don't." He rose then and walked off and didn't look back and I knew that he expected never to hear about it again.

I remembered most vividly his hands on my shoulders. My father's hands were strong and broad and calloused; he hoisted his share of the world's crushing loads. Still, his hands seemed gentle. Hob Farnum's hands were as hard and lumpy as the knots in oak logs, horny and chipped. It seemed to me that they must always be cold, like frosty iron.

It was a time of brutal misery for me. I had chickened out of the fight with Burrell and now he and his father held me in mocking contempt. When I went out to work with them, they would fling casual insults at me and now and then a careless blow. That was rotten, but it was worse when I was alone with my thoughts, sunk in the full conviction that I was a yellow coward. That's all I was; I was born that way and there was no way out. I had often imagined that if my cowboy heroes, Gene or Roy or Wild Bill Elliott, ever had opportunity to make my acquaintance, we would get along famously; they would find me a likable lad. But now that I was a coward, they would turn away in disgust. I felt so degraded that I could not even sustain those fantasies of friendship.

"Well, there ain't no way but just to fight Burrell," I said. "No matter what my father says, no matter anything." And I felt relieved when I made the resolution and my spirits lightened.

But I couldn't keep to my resolution. When I went out to the fields with Hob and Burrell, the offhand contempt and cool abuse seemed to offer no clear dramatic opportunity for me to say, "All right, let's go ahead and have it out, you and me." The sentence stayed bottled up in me and ached in my stomach like a wood stove ember and I went about gloomy and despairing. Burrell would say, "Go and fetch the water bucket, I want a drink," and I would set off meekly and return sullen and every step of the way the words throbbed and died in my mouth: Go and get it yourself, you son of a bitch. *But if I couldn't fight, I surely couldn't say the fighting words.*

It was all upside down. They were the tenants and lived in the little weathered house with its bare yard pecked over by listless chickens; I lived in the brick house under the trees. Yet I was the one who was getting bossed around, the one who felt petty and subservient.

The spring wore into summer and still I made no headway with the problem, which loomed larger than ever. Now that school was out I would have to work day after day, week after week, with Hob and Burrell in a continual dull agony of apprehension. It was like a penal sentence.

One morning as we were pouring the milk into the big steel cans for Pet Dairy to pick up and haul away, I tried to

broach the subject to my father. "What would you say if I
was to get into a fight with Burrell?" I asked.

He didn't look up from pouring his bucket. I could smell
the milk and feel its cottony warmth. "Why would you ever
want to do that?" he said.

"Well, I don't want to, but—"

"Then don't."

"But what if I had to? What if he was to start picking
on me, or we had a quarrel?"

"Oh, you've got a quarrel, all right. You had a quarrel
before either of you were born."

"How do you mean?"

"Haves and have-nots." He looked at me now and I
thought that his eyes were tired and his mind seemed fixed
upon a remote subject and not at all upon what we were
saying. "Good Lord, Jess, the Farnums have got troubles
a-plenty without you giving them more."

I wanted to say: It's not like that, you don't understand,
you don't know what kind of fix I'm in. But I didn't say
anything. If I started talking, I'd have to tell the whole
story. I'd have to tell my father that I'd backed down from
a fight because I was a yellow coward.

For now I knew that that was what I was. I began to
keep track of all the little lies I told, all the petty subterfuges
to keep out of petty difficulties, and it was easy to see that I
practiced cowardice every day, all day long, morning till
dark. I knew, too, that there must be other cowardly traits
in me that I couldn't even recognize and a long chronicle of
chickenhearted deeds that I had forgotten.

Once I tested myself. There was a long central rafter that
ran the breadth of the far barn, a shaky four-by-eight
beam about fifty feet long with only one opportunity for a
handhold, the ridgepole brace in the center. I'd often wondered if I could walk across it and now I wanted to attempt
it, if only for the perverse satisfaction of seeing myself back

out of the trial. But I didn't back out. I actually walked all the way across, trembling and swaying for balance and holding my breath and trying not to look fifteen feet below at the cruel iron angles of the hay rake and mowing machine. When I reached the other side, I was sweating and overtaken with a terrible thirst, but I was exultant. My elation lasted but a brief moment and then I thought, So what does that prove? I still haven't fought Burrell. I still haven't stood up like a man.

I grew fatalistic. Well, all right, I am a low-down yellow coward and that's the way it stands and that's all there is to it. I began to see myself colored yellow, a bright lemony light emanating from my body as from the lantern we milked the cows by in wintertime. This fantasy gave me an odd sense of freedom. I began to behave with an easy carelessness, to walk cockily. What difference did it make what I thought or did? Nobody cares what a coward does.

My father noticed the difference in my bearing. "Well, Jess," he asked, "which cowboy are you today? Roy Rogers?"

"No," I said. "I ain't no cowboy."

Roy Rogers wouldn't spit on me.

It had to come to an end, of course. But even now when I think back, I cannot get straight the beginning of the end. Burrell and I fought; we ended our struggle there on the littered floor of the big barn. But how did it start? Did I actually go ahead and say those words? All right now, I've had enough, let's you and me go ahead and fight. I had rehearsed them often enough, but I don't remember saying them.

I must have said something. We fought.

It was an unseasonably cold April day, the sky gray and louring, moving fast with a wind that crooned through the eaves and around the corners of the tin roof. The weather was the same as on that day I gave Burrell the quick thoughtless slap that had set all this unhappy issue in motion.

He hung back at first; perhaps he sensed the gloomy desperation in me and was wary. I walked forward to meet him almost casually. I was thinking that this wouldn't take much time, he'd beat my ass in a hurry and that part of it, at least, would be over. I was a yellow coward; I could feel the glow of yellow light around my body as I raised my bony fists.

It was the dead conviction of my cowardice that made the difference. Burrell was striking hard sharp blows that should have stung. He hit my face and neck and shoulders. But when his hands entered the heatless yellow aureole around my body, the force went out of his punches. I felt the blows as no more than accidental knocks I might have gotten while jostling a fence stake into a posthole or in wrestling a calf into a narrow stall. I knew that his punches landed—sometimes I could even see them hit my chest or shoulder—but I wasn't hurt.

I fought back without hope or fear. I struck at him only because I knew that if I didn't try to hit him, I wouldn't think of it as a real fight later on and then I would have to go through the whole ordeal again. I was going to lose the fight; he was going to whip my ass good. That was nature's way with the coward. Every Saturday the cowboy movies foretold my fate.

So I punched at Burrell's face in a steady mechanical fashion, rather as if I was trying to drive a nail into a stubborn green oak board. I paid no attention to his attempts to dodge and parry, simply throwing my fists at his face time after time. I was surprised to see that his face and neck and forehead became raw and red, to see that his lower lip had split over the teeth and had begun to bleed. It was amazing to learn that I could make Burrell bleed and

*my attention fixed on this strange red flower blooming in
Burrell's mouth. I hit at that broken place again and
again.*

*Finally, Burrell stepped back away from me. He held his
hands open, shoulder-high. "Lay off a minute," he said.
"I want to rest up."*

*"Rest all you want," I said, but my words seemed to
come out as breathless squeaks.*

*He sank slowly to the floor of the barn, his feet straight
out before him on the thin matting of gray-green alfalfa
stems. With his left hand, he touched gingerly his lower lip,
while his right hand fumbled in the hay.*

*I saw that he was reaching for a heavy piece of broken
tobacco stick, so I took two swift strides forward and kicked
him hard and square in the chest. "Leave that damn thing
alone," I said. "You got to fight fair."*

*He jerked his hand back. He looked at the blood on the
fingers of his left hand. Then he shook his head. "You've
whupped me good," he said. "I'll say Calf Rope."*

"I don't care what you say," I told him.

*"When my daddy hears you've beat me, he'll lay into
me for sure. He'll wear my hind end out."*

*"Don't tell him anything about it," I said. "I wish I
was a big enough man. I'd whip him, too. I'd wear him
out."*

*Burrell stared at me wide-eyed. He knew that he was
looking at a crazy person.*

*But I knew what I knew. The thoughts were as sharp in
my mind as pistol shots: I wish I was grown up now already and owned me a farm with some poor folks on it. I
wish I had me some tenants on a farm. I'd whip their ass
three times a day.*

Six

THE

MEMORIAL

He pushed on the center of the panel several times, gently but rapidly, and could hear the muffled click of metal on metal. There was at least one latch holding it. So he put his eye to the crevice on the left-hand side and, gradually kneeling, followed the line of light down toward the floor. About navel-high, he found the little bar of shadow cast by the latch on the other side, but he couldn't tell what sort of latch it was. Out of habit he patted the pockets of his overalls, but he'd already noticed that his faithful Boker pocketknife was missing.

He'd left it in his suit pants when he changed clothes, or he'd lost it in the creek swimming after that little girl.

What he needed was something to squeeze the bolt over to the right. Didn't need to be much; the plywood panel was only a half-inch thick. If he had a fifty-cent piece—but he didn't. Then his fingertips brushed the hard little rectangle and he drew from his pocket the medal that he had had to choose, the medal that honored Lewis Dorson.

Here was a dilemma. To get the medal to fit into the crack, he would have to press flat the little eyelet that received the pinpoint. He didn't like to do that; it seemed almost an act of vandalism, of desecration. He decided to go ahead and flatten it; he could bend it back again later, no one would notice. He felt, though, a twinge about his heart-root.

He knelt and inserted the medal and began jimmying the latch, working the hard rectangle from side to side until he felt the bolt begin to squirm and ease back. There now, it was coming along dandy. Joe Robert Kirkman could have been a headline success in a life of crime if he'd so chosen; he could have become an expert cracksman, another Jimmy Valentine. When he felt that the bolt was free, he stood up and pushed the door open and entered. He slipped back into his pocket the medal that he couldn't help thinking of as damaged.

What kind of room was this? My father had broken into it because he'd suspected that it was something the students had tacked together. A secret clubroom, maybe, or a place to play cards and trade the indecent funny books, the "eight-page novels," and to smoke cigarettes.

But it was obviously no sort of place that students would construct. A kerosene lantern hung from a hook in the webby ceiling by a strand of seagrass twine and shed its yellow-orange glow and drowsy odor all through the dim spaces here. On the right-hand side, the bulk of the furnace, its ducts and the jumble of lower pipes, took up most of the room. The pipes and ducts led into darkness, into areas my father knew nothing of, had never thought about. Directly beneath the lantern was an unsteady card table with a sagging cardboard top. No part of school property, it had been rescued from a refuse heap and brought there.

On the left-hand side was only more basement junk room in shadow. Broken desks and chairs perched precariously on a belt-high stack of gypsum board. Scattered around were cardboard boxes containing God knows what, and a black grainy dust lay over it all. Dark and cluttered and boring on that side.

Here in the glow of the kerosene lantern, it was more hospitable. Two sturdy-looking steel folding chairs sat beside the card table, though only one of them seemed to have been much used. On the table were a folded stack of newspapers, a pair of scissors with the point broken off one of the blades, and a dented hubcap set upside down to serve as ashtray for a half dozen rancid cigar butts. There was also a deck of thumbed-limp playing cards, damp and grimy.

Uh huh, my father thought. He knew whose little old hideyhole this was. The cigar butts gave it away.

Also on the table was an empty tinware water cup and he picked it up and sniffed the faint but unmistakable smell of corn whiskey that had filled it not so long ago.

And that's the absolute clincher, he thought. This is Jubal Henry's place he has made in order to be somewhere else when he doesn't want to be found, to be out of reach sometimes of those teachers who are always calling upon the janitor to come fix some little old piddling something or other in the classrooms. My father looked around, expecting to find a cot of some kind or a pallet, some arrangement whereby a hardworking man might catch a fleeting forty winks when opportunity arose.

What he found instead was a picture gallery. On the long plywood wall behind him were dozens and dozens of photographs scissored from newspapers, and where there weren't photographs were clipped news stories. Most of them were old and yellowing, but when he looked closer he saw that part of the color was due to the fact that many of them had been painted over with shellac. They had been pasted flat to the wood like advertising bills and then shellacked in an attempt to preserve them. He noted that the clippings were not current and he turned back to look at the papers stacked on the card table. The freshest one was two years old, Friday, Feb. 11, 1944.

He turned around to look at the wall again. There was but one subject for all the pictures and the stories. Here stood a war wall, covered not with pictures of slaughter or of the murderous great machines, nor with maps with their curved black arrows, nor photos of ruined cities, nor accounts of massive victories and defeats. The wall was simply one long sheet of obituaries, the notices and images of the fallen.

It stretched all the way across the boiler room and must have been a good twenty feet long, at least, and already fifteen feet of it had been filled. It commemorated many; the clippings never overlapped; they were laid on neatly but crowded tightly together. There were already scores of notices here and it was obvious that there were more to come, that Jubal Henry was going to fill up every last inch of space.

Looking at the wall my father struggled with a welter of dark emotions. At a distance of twelve feet or so, his eye could no longer make out significant detail, the features of the faces, the names in the headlines; there was only a tangled strong confusion. It reminded him of aerial photographs of battlefields: At first you saw nothing but broken lines and shadows, dark grays and lighter grays. Then little by little, you could make out hill and gulley, trench and bomb crater; and then if you bent close, bringing your nose to touch the glossy acid-smelling print, burying your face in that mud, you could see the twisted lumps that were dead men, transformed by battle into mere mineral figurations of the tortured landscape.

Slowly then, he approached the wall from that distance, one step at a time, and the details clarified: names he could read, faces he could make out. Names he did not want to read, faces that he dreaded to make out. They were distant kin and students and friends and friends of friends and sons and daughters of friends and nodding acquaintances and young men and women he had heard about and had forgotten again until now. They were people, too, that he had never heard about or heard of, complete strangers. Except that now they were all strangers; they had undertaken a mode of existence that made them distant and alien, so that even those he had known closely were as foreign as those he had never met. Yet that wasn't correct, either, because now even the ones he had not known began to seem to have been known, to be part of his life he was just now recalling, and the stranger faces there under their overseas caps and with their arranged smiles came to be faces he had hailed friendly on the street corner or in the byroad for decades gone. The known and the unknown melted together in a single community even as he stepped closer and could read the names of Robert Underwood, Joseph Bowen, Jr., Harley Troutman, Richard Manley, John Morning Bird, James Macclesfield, Johnson Gibbs, Roberta Qualley, Slattery O'Connor, Dennis Gardenia, Kelly Epps, George Washington Carver Flagg.

There was no discernible order in the mounting of the clippings; it was a flat democratic confusion, male female black white indian rich poor catholic protestant atheist schooled illiterate wise funny dull clever human human human human. Nor were the clippings in chronological order; on the right-hand side of the wall, where stories were still being installed, there were clippings of earlier date than on the left-hand side where they commenced.

"Hey. What you doing in here?"

When my father heard the voice, he didn't turn round; he was transfixed by the wall and couldn't tear his gaze away yet. "It's just me, Jubal. I didn't come to bother anything."

"Look around here," he said.

My father turned slowly, all in a trance.

"Okay then if it's only you, Mr. Kirkman," Jubal said. "But I don't want none of the kids finding out this place to come messin' about. I'm going to shut the door here, if you don't mind." He stepped past my father and pulled the panel closed. He had to fiddle with it in order to snap the latch because, with only two small hinges on the other side, it wasn't anywhere near plumb. "There now," he said.

"There now," my father repeated. "There now. Well now. I'm surprised by all this, Jubal. I didn't know there was any place like this down here."

"I didn't care for you to know," Jubal replied. "What you doing down here anyhow?"

"Just happened to be in here with Sandy Slater. Found this room by accident after he left. Even Sandy doesn't know it's here and we spent a good hour talking right in front of it."

Jubal took his constant unlit half-cigar from the corner

of his mouth. The hanging lantern smeared candles of
orange light on the lenses of his gold wire-rimmed spec-
tacles. "You going to be telling him about it?" His voice
was gruff and grumbly, but that was no sign of his dis-
position. His voice always sounded like cinders being
shaken out of a stove grate.

"I don't know. Is there any reason I should be telling?"

"I wish you wouldn't. This is my only place I can get
some peace and quiet."

"That's what I figured, but maybe I'd better find out a
little more. You know me as a fair man, don't you,
Jubal?"

He nodded grudgingly. "I do, Mr. Kirkman, yessir," he
said.

"So you'll be telling me the truth."

"Yessir. What there is of it to tell I will." With his
tongue and lips, he shifted the cigar to the other side of
his mouth, rolling it over as if it were a pine log going
onto a truck bed. His dark skin shone in this warm light
like oiled walnut, but his head trembled slightly and my
father noticed for the first time that Jubal had aged. Impossible to guess how old he was, but he must be sixty-
five at the very least. What hair he had was white along
his temples and down the back of his neck, but hadn't it
always been white? Wrinkles had crumpled the lower
part of his face but without damaging its dignity—and
hadn't he always looked that way? He was like the
school building itself, my father thought. Day after day,
you never took notice until one day you did and said,
This place is so old it's about to fall down.

Not that Jubal was failing. His vibrancy, his wiry ner-
vousness were still sharp; he was still feisty in that way
that indicated to everyone, black and white alike, that he

wouldn't be put upon, that there was a decent distance to be kept between him and the rest of the world.

"Does Mr. Pobble know you've partitioned this basement room off?"

"No, Mr. Kirkman, he does not. You and me is the only ones until you go and tell it around."

"I've got no reason to do that as long as you keep yourself steady. I don't even care if you've got you a little old pot still hooked up to that boiler as long as you don't go selling whiskey or giving it to the kids, or as long as they don't find out some way and come and raid it."

"Who says I've got any little old still down here?"

"I do. I thought you were going to tell me the truth."

At first, he didn't change expression. Then he took the cold cigar out of his mouth and stuck it behind his ear and grinned, showing an impressive set of yellowed dentures. "I ain't denied it, did I? Sure, it's the truth I make a little bit down here. For myself, where it don't bother nobody. I wasn't going to lie to you because I was just about to offer you a taste."

My father pondered. "All right," he said then. "I'll take a thimbleful and no more. Just to see whether it's poison in case some of these kids do find it out. But I can't take a real drink because I've got to teach class in a minute or two and I didn't eat my lunch and I've got to talk to the school board this afternoon."

"Sit you down there at the table and I'll bring us a sup," Jubal said. "I knew you wouldn't drink but hardly nothing. I heard how you have to talk to them board folks."

"You know about that?" He pulled the nearer folding chair away from the table and sat.

Jubal disappeared into the shadows behind the furnace and his voice came out of that darkness thin and hollow. "I heard about it, yessir. I heard that you better step easy with them." He came back into the light again, carrying a quart mason jar three-quarters full. When he came to the table, he unscrewed the lid and poured a good two shots into the tin cup on the table and handed it to my father. "There you go," he said. "If you don't mind drinking after a nigger."

"Now what do I say to that?" my father said. "If I don't drink after you, you'll say I look down on colored people. If I say I don't mind, it's like I've agreed to call you a nigger the way you called yourself. You've got no reason to be shoving me into a corner. I never did you a bad turn, did I?"

Jubal pulled out the chair on the other side of the card table and seated himself with elaborate dignity. "No, you never did, no sir. But ever once in a while, I feel like I want to push back at the white folks and I figured you's the man I could get away with it a little bit."

"You figured wrong. Somebody gives you trouble, you don't take it out on me. You stand up to that man, whoever he is."

"The man that will give me trouble is the one that will just as soon kill me. I rather take it out on you. A little backsass don't do you no hurt and does me a profit of good."

My father picked up the mason jar and opened it. "You gave me too much," he said. He poured half the whiskey in the cup back into the jar.

"If I take a sup now out of that jug, I be drinkin' after you," Jubal said.

My father raised his cup. "Here's to the glory of the primate," he said and they both took a sip, but no more of the nectar than a hummingbird might take from a trumpet vine blossom, and then they gave one another a steady look. "Now we're even."

"No we ain't," Jubal said. "Not never. But we'll get along, you and me."

"I suppose we will," my father said. "We've been together for a pretty good while now."

"You ain't nothing but a newcomer to me. I was janitor here when you was in knee britches; I was working in this school when your mother-in-law taught here."

"How'd you get along with her?"

"I wish we had her back right now. These younguns would learn some respect."

"Gave em what-for, did she?"

"She kep' a firm hand. It's what they needed back then when they wasn't much used to the idea of school, nobody was broke to harness. You teachers now, you got it easy."

My father took his makings out of his bib pocket and began to roll a Prince Albert cigarette. He offered the tin to Jubal, who refused it by taking his cigar from behind his ear and screwing it into the corner of his mouth. "They tell me I've got it easy," my father said. "They don't ask my opinion."

"I can tell you easy," Jubal said, "because I seen how it was before, when they wasn't nothing in this county but three one-room schoolhouses. I seen it coming, though, in those days, how it is now when the schools is big and everybody goes to one."

"Predict the future, do you?"

"Yessir, I do, when it's as plain as a jackass on top of a haystack."

"Why don't you try to foresee how I'm going to get along with this school board?"

He held his body still for a moment, his head not trembling nor his hands, and then he said, "All right, I will," and took up the jar and tipped back a good big swallow of whiskey and turned to look directly into my father's face. But my father couldn't make out Jubal's expression because the lantern light reflected on his glasses blanked out his eyes, making him look like a dead man with gold coins in his sockets. Then his mouth tightened and then, as if he were feeling a sharp pain, his hands lying on the table tensed and clutched at nothing. In a few seconds, something had swept over him and through him, and then he relaxed and leaned back in the chair and spat out crumbs of the cigar he'd bitten down on.

"Are you okay?" my father asked.

Matter-of-factly: "It's going to turn out exactly the way you tell it to turn out."

"That's a comfort. I'm glad to hear I'm not going to lose my job and starve to death." He took another tiny sip of whiskey, no more than would fill a demitasse spoon, but it tasted strong to him, filling his mouth and head with savor and smell and a pure gold color, the color of the light on Jubal's glasses. There was something unsteadying in this underground noontime, the silent still darkness of the basement, and the names and faces of the dead peering over his shoulder, and Jubal trembling again before him like a leaf caught in a spiderthread. It was a different world.

"All right. If you want to hear it how I didn't say."

"You said it would turn out like I told it to."

He nodded.

"Well, there's no question how I want it to turn out."

"Then you must be satisfied."

"Sure. Of course. By all means. Why not?"

"I don't say not. I say it'll turn out just exactly the way you tell it to, and now it's been said three times, so it's bound to come that way."

My father felt himself on the ragged end of this exchange. It was as if he was counting a handful of coins over and over again and arriving at a different sum each

time. He passed his hand over his face, which was as
tender as the belly of a cat, but his confusion didn't pass,
seemed instead to deepen. "I see, I've seen—" he began
but stopped. He couldn't find an order for his words.

Jubal, still eyeless, turned toward him across the table.
His elbow nudged the deck of cards lying there and
spread them out in a tidy fan, except for a single joker
that pitched to the floor. "What you see?"

"I see on the wall here all these newspaper clippings
you've put up. Some of them are old newspapers from a
long way off. I see New York and Kansas and Dallas."

"I've got a buddy at the city dump to save them for
me. They get papers out there from all around the world,
near about." He bent and picked up the joker and laid it
on top of the deck. "These are some people killed in the
war, is all."

"Yes. I recognize that. But why are you putting them
up?"

"First off when I started, it was only people close to
me," Jubal said. "I lost a grandson and three nephews in
this war and I got another nephew looks like will spend
the rest of his days at the Oteen Veterans Hospital. And I
didn't have no proper pictures of them, no family photographs, so I cut these stories out. Then I would read
more and more about boys I know, younguns I would
know in this school here, know some of them better
than a lot of the teachers would. So I started putting up
the writing about them. Then there wasn't no reason to
stop. Everybody getting killed, some mama or daddy
somewhere had lost somebody and they felt as low
about it as I did, and I put up these pictures I didn't
know, too. Everybody was all in it together."

"Yes," my father said. "It seemed like it would never
get over with."

Now Jubal turned his back on my father and looked

off into the shadows behind the furnace. "It won't get over with," he said. "Not in my lifetime and not in yours and not in our childrens' and grandchildrens'. This is to be the war that never gives up."

"You're not foretelling the future again, are you?"

"If that's what you want to say. You see that Chevy hubcap on the table there with them cigar butts in it?"

"Yeah."

"Well, I am foretelling that there is a hubcap on the table with cigar butts in it."

"I don't understand."

"Yes," Jubal said, "you don't."

"You are close onto too ornery to put up with today. You must've got up on the wrong side of the bed."

"I get tired of you not having no proper understanding of things, and I ain't the only one. You got better sense than you use and there's no reason you shouldn't take the blame for that. You listen and you don't hear nothing, you look and you don't see. You see that wall there and you think it's just a little doohickey plyboard partition I've tacked together. What if I was to tell you it was that wall that was supporting this whole building, that this old school would purely fall down if it wasn't that wall there?"

"I'd have to dispute your word," my father said. "It's too weak to hold anything up. And you've just got it nailed to the inside of the joists. It's not supporting the ceiling; the ceiling is supporting it."

"You look," said Jubal, "but you don't see."

"All right, okay. You're preaching some kind of message at me, I can tell that much. So—if I were to see, what would I be seeing?"

"Fire."

"Come again?"

"I mean that the big things, the things important in

your life, will come to you all clothed in fire. That is the way they are to be revealed to you. Like they have been already, only you did not see. But now you had better look to see and when these things are all come over with a cloak of fire, you'll know they have been revealed to you as a sign."

"What sort of things are going to come cloaked in fire?"

Jubal gave him a look of perfect disgust. "How the hell I know that? These here is your signs we talking about."

"Yes, but I don't want to miss them," my father said. "What are they?"

"Ain't no way for me to know. They are personal and different for every man they come to. Even if I could know, I wouldn't tell you. You have to find out for yourself."

My father picked up the cup. There was only a dewdrop of whiskey left in it, but when he spilled it on his tongue, it roared in his head like an enormous red lily full of hummingbirds. "Fire?" he said, but it was difficult to talk. "What kind of fire? You mean like in the lantern here?" He pointed to where it hung steady above the table on the yellow twine.

"Not like that," Jubal said. "Like the fire that's in the lantern when the lantern goes out."

"When it goes out, there's no fire in it at all."

"Only just the fire that gives the best light to see by."

He was irritated now and he wanted to halt this dialogue that seemed only a maze of conundrums and secret formulae. He stood up. "Let's turn this lantern out, then you show me." He turned the wick down slowly and the orange light around them drew into itself like a flower folding at sunset. Jubal watched him without moving as he turned the screw all the way until there was nothing in the lantern but a glowworm line of red

spark across the wick and then a puff of black smoke and
then darkness.

Then it was lightless as a basalt tomb and the darkness
spread out from this one place to engulf all the boiler
room on both sides of the wall. My father heard himself
breathing but no other sound, and he felt foolish when
he spoke in the dark. "Now I'm waiting to see the other
kind of fire, Jubal." But his mockery sounded graceless
to him and without point.

Jubal didn't answer and after long moments the silence began to be unnerving. "I'm still waiting to see
that other light," he said, but wished he hadn't. Jubal
made not a sound, not even the involuntary noises of the
human quick.

"When do you reckon this other fire will show up?"

The darkness and silence were too eerie, so he took a
penny box of matches from his bib pocket and struck
one of them. He held the match above his head away
from his eyes. He could make out little at first but saw
clearly that Jubal's chair was empty.

"Jubal?"

He reached for the lantern but it was no longer before
him. Just before shaking out the match as it began to
burn his fingers, he caught a glimpse of the lantern high
up; it had been hoisted to the spidery ceiling out of
reach. Then in the blackness he asked again: "Jubal?"
But he knew that the old Negro would not answer, that
he was carrying out some crazy private plan my father
was helpless against and, for the moment at least, would
simply have to live through.

The only thing to do was to get out of the basement
without falling over something and breaking his neck.
He'd better hurry along about it because he was already
late for his class, and he didn't have the excuse that he'd

thought he would have, of finding some students up to
mischief.

He felt behind him with his foot to try to get his bearings but couldn't find his chair. It sounded as if there
were six or seven matches in the box when he shook it,
so he lit another and discovered that the little area
around him was empty. The folding chairs were gone
and the card table and the hubcap ashtray that had set
on it. The silent emptiness made the surrounding darkness seem even darker.

He held the match before him and walked carefully
toward the wall, so carefully that he might have been
going tiptoe, but the match burned down before he
reached it. Except that he never reached it. He came to
the place where he thought it ought to be and struck
another match, only to see once again that there was
nothing there, that the wall, too, had disappeared.

He was confident that he wasn't lost in this sightless
basement; his sense of direction unerring. This was the
spot; it was just that the wall with its faces and voices of
the dead was gone. He thrust his hand forward and
there, just there where the wall had been, was a place of
icy coldness. The basement itself was cool enough, but in
this one area the temperature was of Arctic intensity.

That was another frightening part of the episode, but
at least this coldness showed him that he was going in
the right direction. He reached forward to right and to
left and encountered the same icy touch, like a slash
with a frosty razor blade—so that he must suppose this
coldness ran the whole length of the absent wall, and
that there was no going around it.

He lit another match—and confirmed what he had already guessed: that the frozen darkness before him was
also opaque, that the light of his match would not illumine it.

So that there was no other way but to go forward through it, which, as he cheerfully and silently admitted, he dreaded to do. But since there was no choice, he readied himself, clenching his fists and holding them straight out before him, and gritting his teeth, and closing his eyes against the unfriendly dark. The most important thing, more important than any danger, was to get out of this damned basement boiler room that he wished he'd never seen or known of. He could never have imagined before this hour that he could hate a single room so much.

He marched straight ahead and received the shock through his whole body, head to foot. It was like passing through a curtain of shadow from intergalactic space, and maybe that was what it literally was, because there was no air to breathe in that brief place but only the coldness that at first was as sharp as spear blades and then so numbing that his body thought he had died and so told his mind that he was dead.

Then he was on the other side, in the basement proper, where he had held—it seemed a very long time ago—colloquy with his friend Sandy Slater. It was dark on this side too, but enough light fought in through peepholes and crevices that he could see the size of the room and the furnace and the stairs leading up. A warm relief washed all through him and he breathed like a man rescued from drowning in the ocean.

He marched on some six or eight feet before turning to look behind him at the curtain of onyx shadow—which was no longer there. It was once again a partition of ordinary plywood and my father nodded and muttered, "Of course. Of course."

He thought that he was only angry now and not frightened as he made his way slowly and with a fine exactness up the creaking wooden steps. But then when he reached the metal exit door, he found that he was wrong about that too, because he had difficulty unclenching his right hand to take hold of the knob. And when he did open his hand, he found in his palm a wet pulp of cardboard and sulfur-smelling splinters where he had so tensely crushed his matchbox.

Seven

BACCHUS

When he stepped through the steel door into the rational sunlit life of the upper world, he fell into confusion. The light dazzled him for a moment. Then came a sensation of fresh relief, a feeling as of being unwrapped from his winding sheet and given over naked to the blue sky of Maytime. But he had no peace to analyze this feeling or even to enjoy it, for when he climbed the four steps up into the cindery schoolyard, he heard his name shouted out and briefly formed the impression that he had been inducted into a loud game already in feverish progress.

"Catch him, Mr. Kirkman, he's coming to you! . . . Aw, dadgummit, you let him get away."

And indeed he had let the animal escape, startled into immobility as the creature with a bilious yellow glance and what sounded like a loud mocking snigger streaked past him and clattered down the steps into the cramped cul-de-sac there at the green basement door. Then, finding itself enclosed, it showed a flash of panic, or of genius, and reared right around and charged back up the steps, brandishing its short curved horns in comical threat, and shoved past my father out into the yard once more.

"Oh *no*. Mr. Kirkman, you let him get away again!"

It was Billy Joe Pressman who was excited enough to voice his exasperation with the teacher. He was overwhelmed by the thrill of the chase. My father felt that he could hardly take Billy Joe to task. After all, it was the thrill of the chase that accounted for his own striking personal appearance on this day of days.

"How come you boys are chasing this goat, Billy Joe?" my father asked.

The lad looked at him in astonishment. "Everybody's chasing him," he said. "He's been running us ragged."

My father looked about to observe that the schoolyard had, in fact, become a sort of dramatic arena. Students and teachers alike were crowded to all the windows on this side of the building to watch while five other boys began to advance upon the goat as it backed slowly toward a corner. The spectators would witness, my father thought, a scene of teasing futility, for though it looked as if the five might be on the verge of capturing the animal, that was mere deceptive appearance. He had had opportunity to study the manners of a fair number of goats over the years and he recognized in these bright yellow eyes the glint of cunning and he knew that this

goat overmatched in intelligence his nice awkward ado-
lescent boys, all shoulder blade and elbow and lumber-
ing feet, as they converged and as the goat lowered its
head and raked the cinders with its left-front hoof.

He was a handsome animal, slender and rather tall
and piebald white and tan, gleaming in the sunlight. He
was a well-cared-for goat; it was easy to imagine him the
darling pet of a young farm girl, escaped from his pen to
make a holiday of mischief.

"He seems like a nice enough goat," my father said.
"Why don't we just leave him alone?"

"Mr. Pobble told us we had to catch him," Billy Joe
said. "He got into the schoolhouse and went tearing
through the halls and some of the classrooms. The girls
were all screaming and everybody got all in an uproar.
So we need to catch him and take him back where he
came from."

"Where did he come from?"

"Don't nobody know," Billy Joe said. His voice was
full of joy and wonder and his face shone with happiness. It was clear that the arrival of this goat upon the
shores of public education was the most interesting fact
of Billy Joe's young life and that he hoped every day of
his future would be as newsworthy as this one.

"Well, he's not a wild goat out of the forest. He's
wearing a name tag."

"Can't nobody get close enough to read it. Except it
looks like we're about to get hold of him now." His
voice saddened; the adventure was about to end.

"I don't think so," my father said as the boys attempted to spring upon the goat all together at once and
succeeded only in literally knocking their five heads with
such force that they rebounded and fell flat on their
backs into the cinders. They formed a ragged sunburst
design, lying in a circle with their feet pointing toward

the middle where the goat stood untouched and in a perfectly collected state of mind. It found their prone figures no let or hindrance as it picked its way over and past them and took up a new station near the center of the schoolyard, a position that gave it vantage to escape in almost any direction. There it waited, curious to see what other entertainment these young men had planned for this hour and probably hoping that when their performance was concluded, refreshments would be served.

"I'm not absolutely sure that you fellows have lit on the winning strategy," my father said.

Billy Joe gave him a look of which the tacit import was: Everybody thinks he's a born critic; yet he answered politely enough. "He's a slippery cuss, all right. But all you can do is just grab hold and hang on."

"It'll never work."

"Well, how are we going to catch him? What would you do?"

"You have to reason with him."

"How you mean, reason?"

"You must use your powers of persuasion," my father said. "If you convince him that your idea is the better one and ought to prevail, he's bound to act in accordance with your desires. That's only common sense."

"But what if this goat ain't got no common sense?"

"Then he's the kind of goat your mother wouldn't want you to associate with and you must stop chasing him altogether."

The five luckless boys picked themselves up and examined their pants and shirt-sleeves to see what damage the cinders had inflicted. Two of them found jagged tears and became a little angry, more seriously determined now to capture this goat.

They turned their attention to it and it seemed that they, too, had grown more cunning. Without speaking, without signals of any kind that my father could observe, they casually separated from one another and walked away—as if each of them had recollected a previous engagement in a distant place. There was an ostentatious insouciance in the way that they carefully did not glance at the goat. Then when they had got fairly far apart, they turned without seeming to turn and began to stroll— each of them perhaps whistling the same silent tune— toward one another. The semicircle that their steps more or less described more or less centered the goat within its arc. It was a piece of ensemble movement worthy of a Parisian ballet troupe.

Yet it did not much impress the goat, which angled its head from side to side, aiming a suspicious eye now at two of them and now at the other three, and jerking its efficient-looking horns up and down. It watched them confidently as they began to draw toward it and then, when they were a bare few feet too far away to make a concerted rush, it turned its hindquarters on them and walked off, precipitating a soul-sinking anticlimax. My father read sympathetically their expressions of disappointment and frustration.

"Go ahead and give it a try," Billy Joe shouted.

So they made a belated rush, but the animal was too far away. It bounded lightly up the fire escape, taking four steps in its first leap.

"Oh no," Billy Joe said. "Now it's going up the fire escape. Oh no." He groaned the most transparently hypocritical of groans.

"But this is our best chance," my father said. "Once it goes up there, it's got no place else. The only way it can come down is by us. Then we've got it."

The goat's white and tan flanks shone in the sunlight and its hooves made a sound like seductive castanets as they all went up. The old rust-splotched iron structure

trembled warningly. The boys were red-faced and determined, watchful for tricky maneuvers, while the goat
seemed quite relaxed. Billy Joe and my father brought
up the rear, the teacher amused and careful, the student
disappointed that the animal was to be apprehended so
easily.

Up they went. The goat paused at the second-story
landing and glanced behind to see if its pursuers were
still faithful, then climbed again, stopping here and there
to sniff and then to lick the peeling paint.

"Huh-oh," my father said.

"What's the matter?" Billy Joe asked.

"You know how goats eat tin cans—eat anything at
all? We'll be in real trouble if he starts eating up this fire
escape. I'm not sure if it's safe in the first place."

"Nah. He can't do that." He looked into my father's
face. "Can he?"

"We'd better watch him pretty close."

When it reached the third and final landing, the goat
stopped and stood with its front hooves on the last upper
step. It looked around as if searching for a way out, then
peeped behind to see if its entourage was still following,
and then advanced out onto the landing, stepping fastid-
iously, one shiny hoof at a time, toward the steel-sheeted
green fire door at the other end.

Now the boys deployed carefully onto the landing,
three of them in front and three behind, my father and
Billy Joe in the second group. They tried to go as silently
as jungle warriors; they didn't want to frighten the goat
now that they surely had it cornered. There was no place
for it to go farther and no way to get past them.

The goat halted in front of the green door to take its
measure, examined it meticulously up and down and
from side to side, then turned around to face its pursuers.
It lowered its head and tapped its hoof on the iron, clank

clank clank. It shook its horns. It gave them the scornful glance of an embattled Achilles.

They girded themselves.

But it did not charge. It exploded in a high spring, flinging its front hooves onto the top railing on their left-hand side. Then, with a deft half-twist, it leaped in a swift and sinuous motion onto the roof of the school-house.

"Oh *no*," Billy Joe cried. "Now it's up on the roof! We'll never get it down from there. Oh *no*." Easy to tell from his tone of voice that the sight of God in all His glory among the cherubim and seraphim would not equal the sight of this goat on the schoolhouse roof. The life of Billy Joe Pressman had reached its natural climax in his sophomore year of high school and from here on out would be all downhill. Disappointed with his later colorless years, he would, my father surmised, wind up a dope fiend or a literary critic.

They stood and watched then, their mouths open in wonder, as the goat marched slowly to the apex of the roof and stood there outlined against the sky in mas-culine majesty like a storied hero out of the epical ages. The sweet spring breeze moved its beard, swaying the short silky fringe like a banner, an oriflamme, and the sun gleamed bright on its piebald flanks. It was a rare sight to behold and it posed there as if aware of this fact.

"Now it really does present something of a problem," my father said.

"What are we going to do?" Billy Joe asked.

"I think I'd better try to negotiate with it. I'll have to be the one who goes up. Can't have you boys up on the roof, I'm afraid."

"Well, we wouldn't be tearing the shingles off, at least."

Which was what the goat was doing, nipping his teeth

into the edges and ripping the shingles off like tearing
pages out of a Sears, Roebuck catalogue. Already a good
yard or so of felt was exposed. It tried chewing on them,
but something about the taste seemed to anger it and it
spat out a wad of shingle and then returned to its van-
dalizing.

"True enough," my father said. "But you might fall off
the roof and that goat never will. I'm going to have to go
up there."

"How do you expect to get it down?"

"I don't know that part yet," he said. "But it's not
going to come down unless we persuade it that that's the
only course of action that will satisfy us. What I need is
for you to go and find me some stuff for it to eat."

"What kind of stuff?"

"Apples, turnips, tomatoes, rutabagas—anything I can
get it to come to me for. Somebody'll have something.
Try the lunchroom."

"Will you be here when I get back?"

"Give me a holler. I'll be on the roof with Tonto
yonder."

"You think that's his name, Tonto?"

He looked at the goat, which had stopped destroying
the roof and was marching up and down the ridgepole
like a proud sentinel in a beleaguered citadel. "No," he
said, "Tonto's not the right name. You hurry along now
and get me some stuff to tempt him with. We don't want
to waste the whole school day on this goat, do we?"

"Oh *no*," Billy Joe said. "No *sir*." He set off, trying to
look as if he was going fast.

My father walked down to the fire door and pulled it
open. Two boys held it for him as he climbed up on the
fire escape railing, then took hold of the roof guttering
with his left hand and used the top edge of the door as a

step to ease himself onto the roof. It wasn't that hard a climb; he was huffing for breath only slightly.

He rested for a moment, not making any sudden movements. He didn't want to unnerve the goat and he didn't want to tip over backwards onto the fire escape and break his neck. Let us just *festina lente* here, he thought. I have fallen from enough heights today to satisfy me for a good long time.

He stood then and walked, or strolled or sauntered, to the top, keeping a comfortable distance from the goat, which had stationed itself down at the east end of the roof close by the chimney and was eyeing my father with a cool professional skepticism. But he didn't return its gaze and merely walked to the ridgepole to stand by the chimney on the west side with his hands plunged conspicuously into his pockets. They knew what they were about, the man and the goat, in this nonchalant game; they were feeling one another out like horse traders.

So there he stood with his hands in his pockets, having struck the most sophisticated attitude he could muster and looking particularly not at the goat. He looked instead due south, looked down the tall hill and over the town of Tipton, past the river with its farms laid out neat and green on each side of the water and its bordering oaks, all the way to where the Pisgah range of mountains smoldered in blue haze. Cars slid through the sluggish streets and from the paper mill rose the endless gushed smokes gray and black, acrid and sweet and rotten-smelling. He could hear the distant muffled clash and grumble of the freights pulling into the mill terminals and he saw on the right-hand side how the Pigeon River came to the factory bright and clear and poured out below the woodyards as black as the inside of a smokestack and patched with long white stinking streamers of chem-

ical foam. He saw the roofs of stores and houses like the
gray sides of dollar bills and he wondered if anyone
down there might be looking up this way, looking at
him, Joe Robert Kirkman, and wondering what in the
world he was doing on top of the schoolhouse with a
goat when he ought to have been teaching his Civics
class.

And he thought that if he was asked, he might have a
hard time explaining it himself and would only say,
Well, this is one of those days, you know how it is.

He sat down then by his chimney and the goat stood
by his and there they rested some thirty yards apart like
a pair of architectural ornaments. These were evidently
going to be slow diplomatic maneuvers.

The goat made the first move, trotting a few quick
steps toward my father and then halting. He waited a bit
before reciprocating, then scooted on his butt a yard or
so eastward. Thus they approached one another in this
tentative and modest manner like a bashful young cou-
ple courting on a sofa. It took them a good ten minutes
to wind up ten feet apart, with the geometric center of
the roof between them.

My father still gazed off into the misty mountains
when he first spoke. He kept his voice low and soothing,
trying to win the animal's confidence. "Well, son," he
said, "I suppose you're wondering why I insisted on our
meeting up on the roof like this. I want to assure you
that it's all a part of my Big Plan. In the first place, it
gives us a little privacy, you and me."

The goat jerked his head up and gave him a sharp
glance but made no reply.

"I wish I had a turnip or some peppermint drops," he
continued. "I think that would get our discussion off on
the right note. But I don't have anything for you to eat
and to tell the truth, I'm not sure but what I might eat it

all up myself. I'm feeling mighty hungry and that's no joke."

The goat raised his head and sniffed the breeze as if he was finding out whether there were any interesting female goats in the whole landscape to the south of them. Still he kept his own counsel.

"But of course that's my concern and none of yours," me father continued. "What's your name, by the way? I'm finding it awkward to converse when I don't know what to call you."

"Bah-ah-ah-chus," said the goat, drawing the first syllable out like a strand of bubble gum.

My father nodded. "That's a fitting name, a good old classical name. Just suits you. My name is Joe Robert Kirkman, but I never felt that it suited me. The name I like, the one I truly lust after in my heart, is Izambard Kingdom Brunel. But that one's been taken a long time ago. It's too bad we don't get to choose our own names. Did you ever come across a name that you wished you possessed instead of Bacchus?"

"Neh-eh-eh-ver."

"Well, okay, I can understand that. But sometimes I feel like I've been shortchanged. I don't mind telling you, Bacchus, that I harbor such ambitions that a humdrum name like Joe Robert does them no justice."

Then they both fell silent for a while, as if they were already old friends too companionable to feel the need of chat, content to enjoy the weather and the view.

It was, of course, my father who broke the silence. "I don't know, Bacchus, whether anyone has taken the trouble to welcome you to our school, but I'm glad to see you here because you present an opportunity for some of our students. We're in a curious situation with this school located in a mill town in the middle of farm country. There are town students here who probably never saw a goat before. Now that they have, I'll bet they don't forget. So this experience is more valuable to them than whatever they might and might not learn in class. I've got no complaints. I'm pleased that you showed up."

"Thah-ah-ah-anks," said the goat, emphasizing the vowel.

"And Billy Joe Pressman is extremely happy to make your acquaintance. Perhaps you noticed."

"Yeh-eh-eh."

"So up to this point, I think we must count your appearance here at Tipton High School a fine success. It has been dramatic and educational and you have shown a real flair for acrobatic comedy. But I am going to suggest that our rooftop tryst now marks the natural high point of the episode and that if you choose to prolong your visit in this exhibitionist way, our good old mountaineer tradition of hospitality might feel some sense of strain and our sentiments of welcome might well turn into annoyance and finally into rancor. I don't want to be unmannerly, but I'm sure you'll understand that we have some ongoing business in hand with our students, which you have disrupted—quite without meaning to, I'm sure. Nevertheless, I'd like for you to consider the possibility that it might be best to take a final bow and let me help you down from here and return you to the place where you belong."

The goat made no verbal reply but made a motion with its head that might have meant either yes or no, but which my father interpreted to mean undecided.

"Why don't you think it over for a minute or two?" my father said. "I'll go over and see if Billy Joe has got back yet. He might just have a bit of a surprise for us."

He rose slowly, careful not to disturb the animal, and walked easily down to the edge of the roof. Billy Joe was standing alone on the fire escape, holding a brown paper bag. He was still highly excited and my father saw that he was only waiting for a chance to sound out his "Oh no!" once more and attain some higher state of rapture.

"Where is everybody, Billy Joe?" my father asked. "We're going to need some help when I get Bacchus here on the fire escape."

"Is Bacchus the goat's name?"

"That's what he says."

Billy Joe grinned then and said, "Well, don't you see? They're all over yonder on the bank watching you."

My father looked then for the first time and saw, ranged along the top of the high clay bank that enclosed the back schoolyard, what seemed to be almost the whole personnel of the school—teachers, students, lunchroom cooks, and all: a good two hundred people at least, and all looking at him in silent speculation. Good Lord, he thought, how did I get into this fix? But he knew how it had happened and he didn't want to think about it. If I get this goat down from here, he thought, I expect a four-star ovation and a job offer from the Clyde Beatty Wild Animal Circus.

"They gave me some stuff for the goat to eat," Billy Joe said.

"What have you got?"

He opened the bag and peeped. "Got some turnips here and some broccoli and a pretty good bunch of carrots."

"Broccoli?" my father said. "I hate that stuff. I don't think that even a goat could choke down broccoli. Let's try the carrots."

"Here you go." He offered to toss the bag up to him.

"Just the carrots," he said. "The paper makes too much noise. Don't want to scare him off."

Billy Joe gave the bunch of carrots an underhand pitch

and my father plucked them out of the air with a flourish that suggested he was conscious of having an audience.

"Anything else?" Billy Joe asked. "I've still got some turnips."

"If these carrots don't tempt him, nothing will," he said and turned and started back up.

The carrots were, in fact, very tempting to my father. It seemed ages since he'd eaten breakfast and his stomach felt as empty as a basketball. When he reached the ridgepole he sat down in his former place by the west chimney and gnawed on one of the carrots. It tasted wonderful, so wonderful that he began to glutton on the vegetable, munching away like a beaver. When Bacchus evinced some interest in this impromptu snack, my father neglected to show any interest in Bacchus. His hunger had overmastered him. The goat came to him and nudged his left arm with his wet nose and my father responded only by hunching over closer against the chimney. He was so protective of his carrots that when Bacchus tried to steal a bite of one, he actually stood up to keep it away from the animal. He leaned back, resting his buttocks on the top edge of the chimney, trying to stare down the goat, and gobbling his carrot as if it were the last bit of foodstuff left in the solar system.

This turn of events seemed at first to amuse Bacchus, then to puzzle, and finally to anger him. He backed up a few steps, quickly and neatly, and then rushed to give my father a resounding butt on his belly button. My father stopped eating all of a sudden, but before he could recollect his ingenious plan and his best manners, he was thrust heavily back into the chimney. He felt it give way, for this chimney, like the rest of the schoolhouse, was crumbly with age and usage and not suited to rough treatment. Bricks tumbled out upon the roof shingles and down the flue and my father tumbled too, midsection first, down the flue—but not very far.

The result of the blow left my father sitting in the ruined chimney as in a seatless chair. His head and shoulders were vertical enough, but so were his legs. He was tightly folded into the chimney like a hairpin stuck into a cigarette holder and, of course, the first thing he thought about was how he would look at the hearing this afternoon with his clothes even more soiled than before. Now my ass is black! he thought, and in his misery he couldn't help borrowing Billy Joe Pressman's expressive phrase. "Oh *no!*" He said it aloud.

He tried to wriggle free but it was hopeless. He was good and stuck and had even dropped the bunch of carrots. He couldn't see them anywhere and concluded that they must have rolled off the roof or dropped down the chimney since Bacchus wasn't eating them.

In fact, the goat was doing nothing at all but gazing at my father in silent accusation. It was clear that Bacchus was unhappy with the whole episode, that he wasn't even enjoying my father's present predicament. He seemed utterly disdainful.

Yet he was the only aid near at hand. My father thought, If I can just get him to come over here and catch hold of his collar, why, he'll naturally back away from me and might just have enough strength to pull me out of this hole. He realized that it was a frail hope, a remote possibility, but he determined to give it a try.

"Well, Bacchus," he said, "you can see how I'm in something of a fix here. How about giving me a helping hand? We're not enemies, you and I. You might even say that we are well on the way to becoming friends. And you surely wouldn't begrudge a friend in need, would you?"

Bacchus gave my father a slit-eyed level regard. "Oh, we can be better than friends," he said. "Why don't I come over there and give you a big sloppy French kiss?"

"I beg your pardon," my father said.

"I've had my eye on you all afternoon," the goat replied. "And I must say, you are about the cutest thing I've seen in trousers."

My father understood at last. This goat was no innocent runaway, he was a decadent aesthete; he was no embattled Achilles, he was Oscar Wilde. My father prided himself on his talent for improvisation and his ability to get along with every sort of person, but this situation was well beyond the boundaries of his normal experience, and he cast about dizzily for a strategy to deal with it. "I'm sure you'll think this an odd time to ask this question," he said, "but have you ever run across a book called *The Well of Loneliness*?"

"There are some, I think, who would consider your question condescending," Bacchus said. "But I don't mind. In fact, I did come across that book some years ago and devoured it from cover to cover. Not very nourishing, I thought, rather evasive and lightweight."

"Oh," my father said.

"But now," said Bacchus, "enough of this literary chitchat. Let's get down to brass tacks, you and I."

"Oh *no*," my father said.

Eight

SOCRATES

"No," George Ward said. "No no no, no *sir*."

"No sir what?" my father asked. He stood before his class in World History, preparing to talk about the death of Socrates. The ancient philosopher was one of his grand private idols and he had been looking forward to this class throughout the whole school year. He had begun the hour with a story, as he often did, and it was to some detail of this story that his student so strenuously objected.

"I don't believe it," George said. He was not obstreper-

ous and it would never have occurred to him that he might
seem insubordinate. He was only possessed by the clarity of
his convictions and it was the intensity of his convictions
that caused him to speak out so firmly.

"What don't you believe?"

"About this here goat, this Bacchus, him talking to
you like that."

"Surely you don't dispute the evidence of your own
eyes," my father said. "You saw me up on the roof nego-
tiating with the animal. You saw how I treated him like a
real gentleman and how shamefully he treated me in return. You can look and see how my nice new overalls
are all soiled and torn. What is there to doubt?"

"I believe that part. We could all see that part going
on. But I don't believe you-all stayed on the roof talking
about philosophy and stuff."

"Why not? Why shouldn't a goat be a philosopher? I
hope that you don't carry a prejudice against goats—or
against philosophers. Some mighty smart people have
numbered these two classes of animal among the true
and necessary props of civilization."

"But goats can't talk," George said. "That's why."

"And that's what philosophers do, is it? They talk?"

"That's what Socrates does. In this book, anyhow." He
thumped his grimy orange-covered textbook with his
knuckles.

"Your point is well taken," my father said, "for in one
of the dialogues—might be the Euthyphro—Socrates de-
scribes himself as a compulsive talker and says that if he
could get an audience no other way he would be willing
to pay people to listen to him. . . . But is that all he did?
Didn't he ever do anything else?"

"He died," George said.

"Indeed he did, and that's what our lesson is supposed
to be concerned with today. But maybe it's helpful to

keep in mind that he had a full and normal life apart
from his philosophic career. He was an active observer
and commentator on politics and civic affairs; he was
married to a woman well known in her time and place;
he distinguished himself as a soldier; and he interested
himself in the education of young people. But then that
was one of the things that got him in trouble. Still, he led
a recognizably stable life; he wasn't just an old crank
who sat around spitting tobacco juice on the coal heater
and rattling off at everybody who wandered into the
general store."

Scotty Vann spoke up then, perhaps for the first time
in this class. He was a fair-skinned blond student who
blushed easily and averted his eyes at jokes or when
class discussions began to verge upon adventurous subjects. His severe stutter was perhaps more painful for
others to accommodate than for Scotty to endure, but it
was his fearful shyness that prevented my father from
calling upon him in class. Sometimes he would volun-
teer, as he did now, raising his hand halfway and blushing scarlet and gazing steadily into my father's face.
"B-b-b-b," he said. Then he stopped and closed his eyes
and waited to begin again. "But that's wh-wh-what he
s-s-s-seems like, though." He opened his eyes and kept
them unwavering; his fingers trembled.

"I'm afraid that I have to agree with Scotty to some
extent," my father said. "At first glance, Socrates seems
no more than a windy old crank whose idea of a good
time was just to get on people's nerves. But there must
have been more to him than that, don't you think?"

"He was just an old crank," Darlene Thomason declared. "That's all the idea I have about him." Her voice
was flat and noncommittal. It was clear that she had
considered the problem of Socrates and had come to in-
flexible conclusions; she would not ever wish to marry

someone who resembled the ancient Greek; she would
not care to have his like in her family on either side,
paternal or maternal. She would avoid his presence in
the Elysian Fields whenever she disembarked upon those
musical precincts.

"What makes you think he was so cranky?" my father
asked.

"He had a chance to get away," she said, "but he
stayed there and let them kill him. You have to be a nut
to do something like that."

"He gives us his reasons for his choice."

"They didn't make a bit of sense. He wasn't nothing
but just a nut."

"Maybe so," my father said. "In his own generation
that was probably what most everybody thought of him.
But maybe we ought to try to understand his motives.
Maybe we ought to try to put ourselves in his place. In
fact, why don't we do that?" He turned and gathered up
the books and papers and pencils from the desk and laid
them in the seat of the swivel chair he'd rolled to the
side. Then he pushed the chair away. "Come on up,
Darlene, and sit on the desk," he said. "You can take the
role of Socrates and the rest of us will take the roles of
Crito and his friends."

"Oh please no, Mr. Kirkman," she said. "I don't want
to do that."

"Sure you do." He beckoned her with crooked finger.
"Please?" She shook her head sadly.

He went down the aisle and took her hand and led her
gently to his desk in the front of the room. "You'll have a
big time, Darlene. Socrates is a barrel of fun when you
get to know him."

It was plain from the way she hung her head that she
doubted the truth of this remark, but my father was feeling jolly about the experiment, confident that he could

bring the class round to see the beauties of dialectic and
the necessity for the examined life. Darlene sat on the
edge of the desk, crossed her bobby socks ankles, and
stared glumly at the floor.

"So here we are," my father said. "We all understand
the situation, don't we? Socrates has been accused of
atheism, of importing strange foreign gods into the traditions of Athenian worship, and of corrupting the minds
of the young. He has defended himself before the court
in his Apology, but all his brilliance and steady common
sense haven't done him the slightest bit of good. He is
condemned to death. His execution has been put off for a
few weeks because of religious reasons, but the hour
draws nigh when he must drink the poison. He is not
guarded and, if he wished, could escape into exile. It is
clear that the authorities, including some of those who
condemned him, would prefer for him to escape. He refuses. His friends come to visit; they try to persuade him
to leave; they implore. He is steadfast. He would rather
die." He clapped his hands softly and rubbed them together. "Okay. Our job is to try to find out why he is so
stubborn, what his reasons are, and to persuade him to
go away with us to another city, to Delphi, perhaps, or
to Corinth. . . . Darlene has taken the role of Socrates, so
please remember not to call her Darlene."

When he fell silent, the room went silent and remained so. The expressions on their faces showed the
students nettled or bored.

"Come on, now. Who has some questions for Socrates? How about you, Hermogenes?" He nodded at Emmet Fitzgerald in the second seat on the left-hand side.

Emmet looked as if he were tasting the name Hermogenes in his mind and finding it repulsive. He paused
a long time before addressing Darlene in a rather sullen
tone of voice: "Well, Socrates, why don't you go off

somewhere else instead of staying here and getting killed?"

Darlene did not look up. She studied the smelly oiled boards of the floor as acutely as if hypnotized by an abyss of abject misery. At last she replied. "I don't know. I guess I just rather die than go somewheres else."

After another millenial pause, Hermogenes pursued the problem. "How come is that?"

Socrates uncrossed her ankles and swung her right foot forward and back in idle vexation. "I don't know," she said. "I reckon that's just the way I feel about it."

My father interrupted. "Wait a minute, hold up," he said. "This dialogue is not the bang-up success I'd planned. We need to work it out a little better."

Then there was a knock on the door, an occurrence so unusual that for a moment no one recognized it for what it was. Then Emmet Fitzgerald rose from his seat with a grateful alacrity and opened the door wide. It was Dot Whateley there.

"Hello, Emmet," she said. "May I speak to Mr. Kirkman?"

"You sure can," he said.

"Thank you." She looked over his head at my father. "Joe Robert, there's a telephone call for you in the office. The caller says that it's important but not anything for you to worry about."

"I certainly appreciate that," my father said. "From here down to the office is a long way to walk when you don't know what you're supposed to worry about."

"It's a Mr. Campbell."

"Virgil," he said. "Virgil Campbell. Well, he wouldn't call unless it was important." He turned to the class. "I've got to talk on the telephone for just a minute. I expect you-all to behave yourselves while I'm gone, and to find out whether we should save the life of Socrates or

not." He handed Darlene down from the desk and indicated that she was to return to her seat. "We'll start all
over with a brand new philosopher. Philip Sutton is
going to be our Socrates. Take your place here, Soc, old
fellow. And the rest of you bear down on him pretty
close. He's a slippery devil, Socrates is. See if you can't
figure out some questions that will cause him to divulge
his secrets." When he was satisfied with the physical arrangement, he said, "All right, I'll be back in just a jiffy.
If any of you-all do anything different from what I said
to do while I'm gone, I will personally call the high sher-
iff of this county to come and visit you at your house at
midnight. Now, are you going to be so good that Santy
Claus himself might be right here in the room taking
down names?"

"Yes," they said. "We will be good boys and girls."

"Very good," he said and left the room and walked
down the hall with Dot Whateley to the office telephone.

He picked it up and said, "Hello, this is Joe Robert,"
and had to hold it away from his ear as the reply came
through. For all his comparative sophistication, Virgil
still followed the country habit of shouting into the telephone.

"Joe Robert," he cried, "this here is Virgil. Virgil
Campbell."

"All right, Virgil," my father said. "I can hear you just
fine."

"Say you can hear me okay?"

"Yes. Real good."

"Well, I'm calling to tell you to expect a visit from a
newspaper reporter this afternoon when your schoolhouse lets out. She'll be coming over there to ask you
some questions for the paper."

"Why?"

"What did you say?"

"I said, How come she is asking me questions?"

"It's an interview," Virgil cried, "what they call an interview. It is questions about that little girl you pulled out of the river this morning. I found out her name is Appleton. Her folks come by looking for her with firemen and policemen and I don't know who-all."

"It wasn't the river," my father said. "It was only Trivet Creek."

"I told them it was a river. That makes it sound better."

"All right then, I will keep an eye out for this reporter."

"There would be a lot more reporters than just Dora Stoner," Virgil said, "only I owed her a favor. She will be the first to print up your brave exploit and then there'll be lots of others later on. But I owed Dora a favor so I told her first."

"I have not done any brave exploits yet," my father said. "I don't want to talk to a big bunch of reporters."

"You would be helping me out to talk to Dora. There is some politics I'm involved in that I will explain to you later on."

"All right, I will talk to her, but I have not performed any brave exploits."

"What's that you say?"

"I said, All right."

"Okay then. I'm going to say goodbye and hang up the phone. So goodbye then and I'll hang up."

"All right. Goodbye." He replaced the lily-shaped black earphone on its hook and turned to Dot Whateley. "I've just engaged in a short telephone conversation with my old buddy Virgil Campbell," he said. "And I feel like I've plowed a half-acre of new ground."

"I understand what you mean," Dot said. "We get a

lot of calls from folks who talk like that to the telephone."

"Yes," he said, remembering.

When he returned to the classroom, to the World History
discussion of the death of Socrates, everything had
changed. The students were no longer in their seats in
straight rows up and down the length of the classroom.
They had pushed the chairs against the walls and were
sitting on the floor or standing in a semicircle fairly close
around the desk. Their postures were easy and relaxed,
even though they maintained a perfect silence. And Philip Sutton no longer was seated in the place of honor as
Socrates. It was Scotty Vann who now perched on the
desk and he, too, seemed gracefully at ease, not blushing
and his shyness gone from him like cobwebs swept out
of a disused parlor.

"I see that you've changed personnel," my father said.
"How is the discussion going?"

"We were waiting on you," George Ward told him.

"You don't really need me. All you need is to think the
problem out and talk about it. See what conclusions you
can reach."

"*He* wanted to question *you*," George replied, nodding
at Scotty. "He said that it was the divine duty of Socrates
to ask questions rather than answer them. And he said
that since you occupy the same position now that he did
in 399 B.C., it would be more instructive to ask you."

"Scotty said all that? That's more than he's ever talked
in his whole bashful lifetime." He grinned at Scotty and
winked.

"Not Scotty," George said. "Socrates."

"Sure thing," my father said. "Socrates it is. Whatever
Socrates wants, I am honored to oblige."

Scotty got down carefully from the desk and walked to the window. He moved with a slow and certain grace and stood looking into the powerful springtime as my father took his seat on the desk.

This is going well, he thought. They have really flung themselves into the spirit of this exercise.

He was startled from these proud reflections by Scotty's first question—or rather, by the first question of Socrates. George was right to insist that it was not Scotty Vann but the philosopher himself who spoke. It was a darker and richer voice than Scotty's, and as opaque as a passage of Plato printed in Greek. The rhythm of his phrasing was steady and meticulous and informed his whole demeanor. He was more voice than body.

That was it, my father thought. It was as if Scotty's body had become merely a vessel for his authoritative voice. It was the principle of the mask. He had heard about afflicted persons whose stutters vanished when they took on the roles of fictional or historical characters or when they imitated others or sang. That was what had happened to Scotty; he had formed such a clear conception of Socrates in his mind that he could step into the role full-blooded. Better and better, my father thought. I couldn't hope for more splendid results. And he knew that it was important for him to play well his own part in the dialogue. He remembered, too, that Socrates himself claimed to be possessed by a demon, a spirit that caused him irresistibly to search out the truth. Why shouldn't the same spirit come to visit Scotty Vann? For a supernatural being of such caliber and integrity, the passage of a few thousand years would be no hindrance.

But he couldn't answer yet. Amused, confused, he had been listening to Scotty's voice and not to the question. Already he was falling behind. "Would you mind asking that one again, Socrates, sir?" he said. "I'm a little dis-

combobulated here, I'm afraid. I'm not used to such re-
nowned company."

Once more came the steady resonant voice, so anoma-
lous to the instrument it issued from. He found it extremely difficult to concentrate upon the words
themselves.

"Is it not true, Mr. Kirkman, that you have violated
the educational traditions of your own town and county
and of this high school by importing into your classes
strange and foreign ideas?"

"I don't know what you mean," my father said.
"You're going to have to make yourself clear. Don't forget that Socrates was a model of clarity and that a part of
the Socratic method involves his getting his respondents
to formulate precise definitions of their beliefs and val-
ues."

Socrates smiled a mild wise smile. "I shall endeavor to
remember how you have described me to myself, and I
will try to make my question clear. Let us approach the
subject in a different way. Is it not true that in your General Science class here in Tipton High School you have
described and have even employed as explanation the
evolutionary ideas of Dr. Charles Darwin?"

"No," my father said, "that is not true. Or not exactly
true."

SOCRATES. Then I will ask you to show me where I am
wrong, for I love above all things to be corrected when I
am in error. You must remember that I am not expert in
these matters as you are and must rely upon you in order
to acquire a true knowledge.

MY FATHER. I have described the ideas of Darwin to my
students and have suggested them as possible explana-
tions of phenomena. That's not the same thing as ap-
proving them or advising others to subscribe to them.

But I did feel that the young folks ought to be acquainted with them, at least.

SOCRATES. You admit, then, that you have broached these ideas in the public classroom.

MY FATHER. Yes. So what?

SOC. Now, would you describe the town of Tipton and the local community that supports this school as places that encourage the understanding of modern science and advocate the enlightened progress of scientific knowledge?

FATHER. Good Lord, no. This is the frozen orbit of Pluto as far as modern science is concerned.

SOC. Do you think of this local community as containing a majority of citizens who would approve of the theories of Dr. Darwin if they could be led to understand them?

FATHER. No. I suppose that they would find them shocking and frightening and maybe blasphemous.

SOC. You have used the word *blasphemous*. May I take it, then, that you discover a strong religious faith to be common among your fellow citizens?

FATHER. Yes, that is certainly true.

SOC. And the ideas and concepts that comprise the theory of evolution are in conflict with the ideas and concepts that comprise this common religious faith?

FATHER. It is my strong personal opinion that there is no basis of conflict, that the religious and scientific modes are two entirely separate kinds of understanding, and that they can reach disagreeing conclusions without genuine conflict or come to identical conclusions without actually complementing one another. Wouldn't you agree with that?

SOC. It is difficult for me to say, for the subtlety and ingenuity of your argument is perhaps beyond the capacities of a simple man like myself. I am, moreover, disposed to argue the point as your fellow citizens might argue it. Do you believe that they would understand and agree with your argument as you have just unfolded it to me?

FATHER. Some of them would understand and agree, others would disagree. I'm afraid that most of them wouldn't understand. To tell the truth, I'm a little shaky about it myself.

SOC. But on the basis of an argument that they would not understand, you seem to feel justified in teaching to their children a theory that their religious principles can in no manner approve.

FATHER. Well, it's not just on the basis of my argument, not at all. The fact is that Darwin's theory of evolution has long been accepted by the scientific community as being incontrovertible in its major conclusions. Science has already absorbed Darwin's theory and gone on to the matter of its details, or to other subjects entirely. There is no way for the kids to catch up with contemporary scientific thought if they don't have some bit of an inkling of what evolutionary theory is.

SOC. Is it then of supreme importance that the students should be conversant with contemporary scientific thought?

FATHER. Only if they want to understand the world they live in. Seems to me that this war we just fought teaches us that science is going to be one of the main driving forces of civilization from here on out. I know that you agree with me in this matter. I know from reading your own words that you believe that knowledge is power and that understanding leads to happiness.

SOC. It is clever of you to quote my own words. I hope, though, that I may be allowed to point out that I spoke of self-knowledge as having power over one's own passions, that I was not speaking of the use of secret knowl-

edge as a weapon against others. This latter usage would
amount to a sort of blackmail, or extortion. I might agree
that broad understanding leads to the possibility of happiness, but perhaps we ought to examine the nature of
the understanding you are thinking of. In this case, we
are concerned with scientific knowledge and theory, are
we not?

FATHER. Yes.

SOC. Would you agree that in science, as in other areas
of human endeavor, there are certain individuals,
thinkers and experimenters, who have been preeminent
in the history of the discipline, men to whom others
turn, gathering the fruits of their efforts and the sanctions
of their authority?

FATHER. Indeed.

SOC. Perhaps you would do me the honor of naming
some of these famous men.

FATHER. Well, let's see. Among the Greeks, there are
Aristotle and Aristarchus and Hero, of course. But there
are scores and hundreds of great scientists to whom we
owe the present advanced state of our thought. Kepler,
Newton, Cavendish, Wegener, Frazer, Einstein, Mach,
Born. One of my personal favorites is a fellow named
William Buckland. The list of great names is a very long
one.

SOC. And in this list of names, that of Charles Darwin
is considered prominent?

FATHER. It will rank among the very brightest.

SOC. And his ideas will agree with those of the other
great scientists who have pondered upon the same subjects that he has studied? Will we find that the thoughts
of Aristotle, Darwin, Lamarck, and your friend William
Buckland are in perfect consonance?

FATHER. Oh no. They don't agree with one another at
all.

soc. That seems odd to me, since we are dealing here with factual knowledge, with physical facts rather than with metaphysical speculation. What is it that causes such divergence of opinion?

FATHER. It is the accumulation of evidence over a long period of time. Data are gathered generation after generation and compared with each other. They are patiently collected, considered, and compared against preexisting theories. Then new theories emerge which conform more closely to the newer data.

soc. You would seem to be saying that the amount of truth in science depends upon its place in history, that the newer a scientific knowledge or theory is, the more truthful it is.

FATHER. Well—in a certain sense, that's correct. The familiar apothegm is that in literature it is best to read the oldest works, in science the newest.

soc. Now, in your present time, in which of the sciences do you consider our knowledge to be perfect and complete?

F. In none of them.

s. What, none? Not in physics or astronomy?

F. No.

s. Nor in meteorology, economics, or sociology?

F. No. Absolutely not.

s. But in biology you will have to say that our knowledge is mostly complete and perfect insofar as we know.

F. Not at all. There are still thousands and thousands of questions to be answered and other thousands of questions we don't know how to ask yet.

s. Why is that?

F. Because we will obtain new data, new knowledge, which will change our opinions about what we now know.

s. Might this new knowledge overturn present theories

and overturn even what are at present regarded as certainties?

F. Undoubtedly.

s. Is there not a possibility that new knowledge may overturn even the conclusions of Dr. Darwin?

F. Well . . . That's a possibility, I suppose. But I think that it's quite a remote one. The structure of interpretation he has founded to account for great masses of data and widely disparate phenomena looks to be enduring.

s. But has not this conclusion been thought true of many earlier theories?

F. Yes.

s. So that you have no real guarantee that the Darwinian outlook is to be permanent.

F. I admit that much. It is the nature of science.

s. Now you have admitted that the scientific theories you support and intend to teach are provisional and perhaps transitory. Will the parents of your students hold that their religious beliefs are also provisional and transitory, or will they not rather hold that the principles and tenets of their religion are eternal and unchanging and constitute the most important kind of knowledge necessary to attain?

F. They will undoubtedly make these claims.

s. You must forgive me then where my logic is faulty, for I have not been able to follow your reasoning. You believe that it is incumbent upon you to teach to students doctrines, which you say are no more than provisional and temporary, to the detriment of doctrines that their parents believe to be inescapable truths. I cannot see how you think you have license to do so.

F. Here now, wait a minute. Hold on. This is not going the way it ought to. Socrates will argue in favor of skepticism and the freedom to discuss and learn about knowledge of any sort, whether it agrees with local customs or not. He won't be arguing *against* the theory of evolution; he'd never do that.

s. But that is just what I feared, that we have made some missteps in our discussion. Have you answered my questions truthfully?

f. Yes indeed I have, but—

s. And do you agree that it is preferable to teach to the young what is believed to be eternal and true rather than what is acknowledged to be transitory and perhaps to be found false at a later time?

f. Well, sure, okay, if you put it like that, but—

s. Then I do not see how you can go one teaching the theory of evolution unless you have set out deliberately to corrupt the students. Yet I am convinced that you would not commit such an act.

f. Hold on just a dadblame minute! I don't have the slightest idea of corrupting anybody. It's just very important that they keep up with modern thought.

s. I was confident that you would not purposely injure the children of your neighbors and friends, and I am pleased to hear that you are going to give up teaching this pernicious doctrine, for it seems to me that by your own admission that is what you are bound in conscience to do.

f. No! *Goddammit, Socrates, you don't understand a thing!*

s. So I have been told many times and I think that the charge must be true. I am willing to give you opportunity to put your thoughts to me in such a clear and forcible way that I must agree with them.

f. What do I care whether you agree with me or not? What the hell do you know about Darwin or anything else in modern science? You want to hear the name of a great scientist? I'll tell you one, one of the best that ever lived. Izambard Kingdom Brunel. He's a true hero of mine. I like to think about him all the time. But I'll bet that you never even heard of him. Come on, 'fess up now. You never heard the name before, did you?

s. I must admit that the name Izambard Kingdom Brunel is strange to me. Yet for his sake, I am a little disturbed to hear that you are one of his admirers. For have you not told your acquaintances for years and years that Socrates the philosopher was one of your heroes and that you hoped to model your teaching methods and even your life upon his example?

f. Yes, I used to say that. But that was before I got to know you personally.

s. And now that you have talked to me in person you have formed another impression?

f. The students are right. What you are is a windy old crank whose only real talent is just to aggravate people out of their minds.

s. But do you not think that the role of the gadfly is salubrious to—

f. Socrates, if you don't shut up, I'm going to give you a fat lip and a black eye and a bloody nose. Stuff that in your dialectic and smoke it.

"Why, Mr. Kirkman," said George Ward. "You ought to be ashamed of yourself."

"Oops," said my father. "Sorry. Philosophy sort of ran away with me there for a second."

Nine

PROMETHEUS

UNBOUND

It was taking him a long time to get to the second floor. The stairs seemed as steep and cold and lonely as the Matterhorn and a chorus of miseries whispered in his mind like a ball of hornets. The doomful hour had come round at last; he was climbing the squeaky center-worn steps to go to Room 202 and face the judgment of the school board. All the livelong day from the earliest hour of the morning, he had dreaded these moments and now they had caught up with him and still he was as unprepared as if he had never dreaded them in the first place.

The building was preternaturally still, almost silent. The school day was over, though there were many students outside, some of them waiting for their buses to take them home, others waiting for the baseball game with Hayesville High School to begin, still others merely passing the time in the company of friends. The cries of the students, their muffled shouts and broken squeals, sounded remotely distant, and my father thought that this was true: The students were distant from him now; they were in another country; they had showed their concern and had come with him in his travail as far as they could, but now the school was given over to the grown-ups, to policy and politics. Science and philosophy had enjoyed their hours of sufferance and had departed. Now had arrived the time of inquisition and— well, perhaps not martyrdom. No, *martyrdom* would be too strong a word.

The sunlight streamed on him white and yellow as he reached the landing and slowly turned to start up the last flight of stairs he might ever ascend in his life as a teacher. His body cast a sharp deep shadow and dust motes drifted in the light about him like dangerous sparks sent up from a subterranean furnace.

He was feeling sorry for himself and that was an emotion almost alien and he did not like the crumbling sensation it imparted to his spirit. What had he done, after all, that was so terribly wrong? He had spoken of a scientific theory that was now nearly one hundred years old. He had described it in outline but not in detail and had given a sketchy account of its history. He had neither advocated belief in it nor attempted to force it upon any person against his will. He had planned to include only one question about it in the final examination. The theory of evolution was not the most important concern of his class in General Science, not at all.

If they'd known about it, I wouldn't have brought it up, he thought. But they'd never even heard of Darwin. So then I had to say something.

And he was thinking of himself no more as Socrates, and no more as a genius like Brunel to change the face of the planet, but as Prometheus, punished everlastingly for having brought the gift of fire to mankind. It was not the first time he had encountered this grandiose comparison, but it was the first time he had done so with such solid conviction and without a twinge of comic shame. But when he realized now what he was thinking, he did begin to feel silly and ashamed and turned his mind and tried to concentrate on the task at hand.

I make a piddling figure of Prometheus, he thought. There are many fine Prometheuses and I don't belong in their company. He remembered Edison and Steinmetz and Lord Kelvin. And yet we strung the electric lines, didn't we, up over Wind Mountain and down into Setback, up Harmon Den and all through Max Patch?

He went over the names of the board members in his mind. Sandy Slater had spotted them coming into the school building and had told him who was attending the meeting. He stood at the top of the steps with all the light behind him and whispered them: Susie Underwood, Ben Meaders, Jack Coble, Irene Macclesfield, Cole Smathers, and Handy Conrad. These were his interrogators; they waited for him behind this door here by his left hand. He could feel their presence there, ominous as the shadows of a childhood bedroom. He invoked the spirits of Democritus and Cicero and Senator Clyde Hoey; he would need every ounce of eloquence and persuasion that he could summon forth. How often he had prided himself on his gift of disarming gabble! Now it would be subjected to a pure and fateful test.

So—no help for it. He took two strides and jerked the door open and entered.

Sandy was right. There they all were, sitting in the desks they'd pulled into a semicircle in the front of the room. They looked up at him with unseeing mild expressions on their faces.

"Look here," my father shouted. *"You can't fire me. I quit."*

Then he backed out of the room, slammed the door, and was gone.

Silence once again reigned in the schoolroom, a silence as broad and patient as a snowfall. For a long time the six members of the Tipton school board stared before them into unlocatable space. Impressions fluttered brightly in their minds and then departed\ nonchalantly, like butterflies visiting a rose garden. Had something happened just now? Had a strange person opened the door to speak to them? They sat pondering in the slow silence, cramped and awkward in the student desks all squeaky and smelly and battered and cracked and gouged with cartoon hearts and ink-black initials. To each of the members the lights and shadows and odors and corners of this classroom brought memories of their high school years, the teary triumphs and soul-shaking gaffes.

There they sat in rapt contemplation. Then the door flung open and there occurred the swift and motley visitation. Then the door clapped shut and blotted that lightning apparition away, and still the board members sat there, as transfixed as sages searching the blue plumbless pools of contemplation.

First to speak was Ben Meaders. He was a gray-faced sharp-featured man, phlegmatic and slow-talking. Now his words came out in thick abstracted tones, as if he was asleep and speaking to his dreams. "Good Lord-a-mercy," Ben Meaders said. "What in the world was that?"

The others turned slowly to look at him. Their movements were as languid and hypnotized as the motions of sleepwalkers; there was a communal reverie over them like a tent of spiderweb.

"I don't know," said Irene Macclesfield.

"Me, either," said Jack Coble.

"It's a conundrum to me," said Handy Conrad.

Then the silence returned to the room and they sat again unmoving, immersed in the perfume of it.

"Well, who do you think?" asked Ben Meaders. "Doesn't somebody have a guess?"

"Joe Robert," said Cole Smathers.

"Who?"

"Joe Robert Kirkman."

"Aw no," said Handy Conrad. "It didn't even look like Joe Robert. Not in the least."

"Well now," Susie Underwood said, "I thought that it did favor Joe Robert pretty closely." Her tightly curled red ringlets were whitening now, but behind her plastic-rimmed glasses, her eyes shone as brightly blue as ever. She was a police judge, respected for the quiet justice of her judgments.

"No-no," Handy said. "It was some trifling kid, wasn't it? Dressed up in funny clothes to play a trick on us. He opens up the door and hollers out some trashy sayin' and runs away."

"What was it you heard him holler?" Cole Smathers asked.

"Well, I don't want to say that. Not with the ladies present."

"Handy Conrad," Susie Underwood said, "you know good and well I've been a police judge for twenty years now. What words are there that you think I haven't heard yet?"

"Well, what he hollered didn't make any sense anyhow. That's why it had to be a kid. Joe Robert would've at least made some sense."

"Well, but what?"

"I'll tell you what I thought," Susie said. "I thought he said, 'Look here, you can't hire me not to quit.'"

"How can you hire somebody not to quit?"

She shook her head. "I don't know."

"I'll say what I thought I heard," Handy said. "Excuse my French, but what I heard was, 'Boogers, you're mired to your knees in shit.'"

"Surely not," said Jack Coble. "What I heard the feller say was, 'Suckers, you are tiring me completely out.'"

"But that doesn't make any sense."

"Why does it make so much better sense with the boogers in manure?" He squeaked round in his desk and essayed an apologetic bow. "Saving your presence, ladies," he said.

"I don't see why Joe Robert would be shouting out any of those things," Handy replied.

"Well, but why do you say it was Joe Robert? I thought we were satisfied it was one of the schoolkids pulling a rusty. Not that I'd put it past Joe Robert, you know how he is. He's a funny fellow."

"He is right amusin' sometimes," Handy said. He turned sideways in the desk to ease his legs. "That's why it wouldn't be him. He'd think of something funny."

"I still think it was him," Cole Smathers said.

"Not by the way he looked," Handy said.

"Well, yes, his face and figure, sort-of. I don't mean the way he was dressed. I never saw such a crazy getup. But that's something Joe Robert might put on for the joke of it."

"Not only his clothes," Jack Coble said. "He had stuff on his face."

"All over his face and body," said Susie. "Strange objects stuck to him. I couldn't easily describe what I saw."

"It was a kid," Handy maintained. "Wearing some kind of clown outfit."

"Tell us what he looked like exactly," Susie said. "Maybe if we each describe him, we can figure out whether it was Joe Robert or not. Who should be here now, by the way. He's already five minutes late."

They all looked at the big classroom clock above the blackboard, the clock they remembered from their school years, with its imposing sharp-edged numbers and its black swordlike hands. As they watched, the minute hand clicked from 3:06 to 3:07.

"Well, he was wearing overalls," Jack Coble said.

"That's right," said Irene Macclesfield. She toyed with a strand of her longish coffee-black hair. She was still a strikingly handsome woman. "Overalls and a green shirt."

"No. The shirt was gray," Cole Smathers said. "And the overalls were black around the waist."

"The oddest thing was that he had paint on his face," Irene said. "He'd painted it black and blue and red."

"And yellow," Cole added.

"I didn't see any yellow," Susie Underwood said. "That was a subtle touch I somehow missed."

"His head was all covered with flour or some kind of

white dust," Ben Meaders said. "I don't know what it
was."

"I could see it just a-sifting off of him," Jack said.
"Like when my wife is making biscuits."

"But he had new shoes on," Ben observed. "Brand-
new brogans. I'd hate to be wearing those things."

"I didn't even think about looking at his shoes,"
Handy said. "There were too many other interesting
things to remark about him."

"Like that wild look in his eye," Susie said. "I thought
he might be just a little drunk."

"A little?" Jack said. "Whoever it was, he looked like
an insane dope fiend."

"Nah," Cole said. "That was just Joe Robert trying not
to laugh. When you're trying to keep a straight face and
not laugh, it makes you look strange."

"Might have been those new shoes," Ben said. "It
would sure show on my face if I was wearing those
things."

"But they wouldn't cause you to pour flour on your
head," said Jack.

"Well then," Ben said, "supposing it was Joe Robert.
Just supposing. Why would he dress up in silly clothes
and put flour on his head and paint his face and come in
here and yell out, 'Sugar, you Campfire Girls are
sweet.'"

"That's not what he hollered."

"Well, whatever he hollered, why would he holler it?
Holler anything, I mean?"

"For a joke," Cole Smathers said. "Just to raise some
pure old Cain. Don't you remember what-all Joe Robert
did last year when he was principal? How he flew that
kite made out of his wife's old silk slip and dared anybody to shoot it down with a shotgun? How he dressed
up in a bedsheet in his history class and told them he

was Julius Caesar? My girl Ida came home and talked about it all night. She said she never would forget what Brutus did to him. She said it was a gory sight to behold."

"If it's a joke this time, it's not very funny," Susie said. "Because we don't understand it. I'd give Joe Robert credit for better. I've heard him when he was quite humorous—even witty."

"Well, but you're going to misfire sometimes, too," Cole said. "Even Jack Benny."

"We didn't hire him to be Jack Benny," said Ben. "What we need is a good principal. This is the same way he got in trouble last year."

"I can't see that he's done anything wrong," Susie Underwood said. "As far as I'm concerned he's not in trouble."

"If you ask me, I think it's the Gwynns that are out of line," Cole said. "Not that I've got anything against them, you understand. But it was settled a long time ago back over in Tennessee how you can teach Darwin in the classroom. Joe Robert is supposed to teach biology any way he sees fit. It's a subject he's well up on, the way he takes after all this newfangled science. This whole matter shouldn't have ever been brought before us."

"I agree with that," Ben said. "But when the Gwynns lodged a complaint, then we had to follow through on it. We don't have a choice about procedure. But as far as I'm concerned, Joe Robert can come in here right now and shake hands with us and then we can all go home. I don't see he's done a blessed thing we can call him down for."

Irene said, "Those are my feelings, too. How does everybody else feel?"

"I'm on Joe Robert's side," Susie said.

"Me, too," said Jack.

"And me," Handy said, "but I would advise him to tread easy when he gets to talking about subjects that might border on religion. People get awful touchous about their church teachings."

"I'm sure Joe Robert knows that," Susie said. "He might not be very religious himself, but he would respect the beliefs of other people. That's just plain good manners."

"Well, he's got to show some sign of religion, living there in that house with Annie Barbara Sorrells," Cole said. "She's bound to talk religion at him."

"Wouldn't you just love to be there at the supper table?" Jack asked. "To hear them two spitting like tomcats? It's bound to make a saint laugh."

"He's late, though," Cole said.

They all looked at the big clock. It showed, with implacable authority, a reading of 3:17.

"If he doesn't come pretty soon, I'm going to have to rule that he's already made his visit and that the extravagant greeting we received is all the appearance he's going to make." Susie drummed her fingertips on her desktop.

"No, now wait," Cole said. "He'll be here in just a minute. He'll be dressed up all spiffy and ready to have the horse laugh on us."

"What we ought to do," Jack said, "is figure out some sort of rusty to pull on him when he comes in. Then he won't laugh so big."

"All right," Cole said. "What do you want to do?"

"I don't know. Let's think about it."

They began to ponder and the big clock with its swordlike hands was the only sound that troubled the dusty silence. The mental strain of trying to devise mischief showed on the faces of the four men and they didn't look at one another, watching the ceiling or the floor. The women sat patiently by.

"Well, Jack," Handy Conrad asked, "what did you think of?"

He shook his head and replied in a deeply dejected tone, "I tell you, boys, I couldn't think of a thing."

"Me, either," said Ben Meaders. "I'm plumb disgusted with myself."

They sat again in glum silence.

Susie Underwood spoke up. "It's hard for me to believe that I'm sitting here with four grown men who are feeling sad because they can't dream up a low-down trick to play on one of their friends. I can foresee a sleepless night ahead for me over this one."

"We could tell him that we've already decided to fire him," Jack Coble said. "That would give him a turn."

"Sort of drag it out for a while to make him sweat," said Cole Smathers.

"I don't think that's much of a trick," Irene Macclesfield said, "to tell a man that he's lost his job and will have to find some other way to support his family. That's just dumb and mean."

"We would only be ragging him," Cole said.

"Irene's right," said Handy Conrad. "It's not much of a trick because it's not funny and it doesn't show any imagination. I never realized how hard it is to think of these kind of tricks he plays. There's more to it than just acting a fool."

"Joe Robert's no fool," said Irene sharply.

Handy glanced at her in surprise. "No, of course not. I never thought he was. But he does act foolish sometimes, you'll have to admit to that."

"I'm disappointed we can't think of a trick to play on him," Cole said. "I hate for him to always have the last laugh."

"Well, let's see if we can't come up with something," said Jack.

"I don't think there's any point in it," Susie said. "The clock says three twenty-five. Joe Robert would never show up this late for such an important meeting. I'm pretty certain that we've seen the first and last of him we're going to see today."

"I still don't believe it was him," Handy said. "He might dress up like a clown to pull a joke, but I can't picture him putting makeup on his face."

Cole said, "What I can't picture is what he hollered at us. 'Stuck here, I'm gonna fly me a fit.' That doesn't make a bit of sense. Joe Robert can do better than that."

"That's not what he hollered," Handy said.

"What was it now that you say he said?"

Handy replied firmly: "I am not going to repeat it in front of the ladies."

"Irene," Cole asked, "you're the only one who hasn't reported. What did you think it was that he yelled out?"

Irene looked at the floor and the wall and the clock, then she looked out the window. "I must have got it all wrong," she said. "I think I didn't understand a single word."

"All right, but you thought you heard something. What was it?"

"Well . . ." She glanced at Cole, then looked away again. "Oh, it's too silly. I got it all mixed up."

"Come on, Irene," said Handy Conrad.

"I thought he said, 'Thou art more lovely and more temperate.'"

"Oh, Irene," Susie said. "You're still sweet on Joe Robert, just like you have been for ten years and more." She looked at her friend in exasperation and mournful sympathy.

Irene sat like a schoolgirl, her feet in the black high-heel shoes flat on the floor, her hands open in her lap. She blushed as scarlet as any poppy in the delirious

Turkish meadows. "Why, I am not, either," she said, and her big brown eyes filled with tears. "What a terrible thing for you to say."

My father was holed up in his favorite hiding place, the faculty men's rest room, smoking a consolatory Prince Albert cigarette. He was sad and frustrated and angry with himself and bluely disappointed.

Now why did I do that? he thought. Ever the diplomat, eh, Joe Robert?

He flicked cigarette ashes into the drain of a urinal and leaned against the wall and closed his eyes. He could hear the noises of play from the baseball field that held the beautiful spring afternoon in thrall, but they sounded as if they were coming from a long way off, scores of miles. The day was bright outside the window, but in the white sunlight there was already the promise of amber. He began to feel a twinge of nostalgia for his high school, even for this building from which he had not yet departed.

I didn't need to behave like a madman, he thought. Those are my friends sitting in those school desks. They're reasonable people; we could have worked something out. I know that they don't want me to lose my job. They're all friends of Cora too, and of my mother-in-law. They've known each other all their lives, and they'd probably do anything in the world for those two ladies, whether it involved me or not.

He opened his eyes and shook his head unhappily.

Not that they've got anything seriously against me. They

just think I'm a pure damfool without the least little grain
of common sense. And they're right about that. Only a
damfool would throw away his livelihood just because he
was too proud to answer a few questions.

He took a last drag on his cigarette, then went to the
lavatory. He turned on the cold water and held his cigarette in the flow until it sizzled out and began to melt.
Then he stepped over and dropped it into the trash can.

Now tell the truth, Joe Robert, he thought. It wasn't
pride that made you tuck tail and run. It was pure-T
scaredyness. That's all the world it was; you were only
frightened and shaking in your boots. The sooner you
own up to that, the sooner you can turn right around
and march in there and talk to those folks the right way
and save your job and feed your family.

He returned to the lavatory to wash his hands. He tried
not to see the spectacle he presented in the mirror, but
he couldn't resist.

Oh *no*. Oh Lord. However in the world can I go back
in there looking like this? They probably didn't even get
a good look at me the first time. Now they'll think I'm
making mock of them. It's pointless to try to patch this
interview up. I'd be better off to pack it in and go home.

But then the more he stared, the more accustomed he
became to the way he looked, and it seemed that he
really didn't look too bad after all, if they'd only give him
a chance to explain everything that had happened to
make his appearance so outstanding.

Let's see, he thought. First I fell out of a tree. Then I
jumped in the creek. Then I sat in a dusty chair. Then I
fell down a chimney. . . . Could happen to anybody,
couldn't it? I mean, it all makes sense if we can go
through it step by step.

Putting the story together in his mind, he began to feel
better. He squared his shoulders and straightened the

front of his overalls and gave himself a cheery broad
smile.

It's a good thing I didn't lose any teeth, he thought.
Then I really would scare them off. . . . Let's see now.
How do I open when I go back? What am I going to tell
them? Say, friends, I'll bet you been asking yourself:
How can I get me an outfit like Joe Robert Kirkman is
wearing? Well, I've got the answer you've been waiting
for. First you find a good-sized poplar tree with a bobcat
in it. . . .

No. Stop it, Joe Robert. Get serious now.

I want to apologize to you members of the school
board for my looking like Bozo and sticking my head in
the door and braying like a jackass and running away
like a fox with his tail on fire.

Huh-uh. Let's don't be hangdog about it. Keep it simple and dignified.

My friends, I promised my pal Sandy Slater that I
would kiss your ass in order to keep my job, but I find
that I'm not willing to do that. Does this leave us at an
impasse?

No no no. You are not even coming close.

Nevertheless, he winked at himself and whistled a bit
of a tune. He'd never been any good at planning ahead
of time and he recalled jauntily his favorite text from St.
Paul: "It shall be given to you in that hour what ye shall
say."

He went out into the hall and began to climb the steps
to the second floor again. But now he went more cheerfully and with a confident stride. What had he ever been
scared of the first time? When had his boyish charm and
gift of gab ever let him down? . . . Well, a few times,
sure, but that was all in the past.

He strode down the hall and paused before the door of
Room 202 to tug at his clothing, to compose his face,

and to strengthen his resolve. Then he rapped smartly and entered.

There was no one there. It was as silent as the dust in a disused silo. The arrangement of the school desks was disordered but that was the only visible evidence that anyone had occupied the room. In the air hung the slowly dissipating scent of the perfumes the women had worn and this vestige of their presence was so ghostly it caused the hairs on the back of his arm to prickle.

It was as if his friends on the school board had been abducted into time past and he would never see them more.

He sat down heavily in one of the desks and looked at the clock above the blackboard. The black minute hand clicked sharply as it moved to 3:36. That noise sounded to my father like a guillotine blade coming down thwack.

Ten

FOXFIRE

All day long, nothing had turned out the way he had thought it would, and the reporter sent by Virgil Campbell was another surprise. Dora Stoner was no gum-cracking, staccato, impatient Joan Blondell, but a soft woman in her late fifties or early sixties. She wore a dark-blue rayon dress that fell nearly to her ankles, and she was carrying a Blue Horse spiral notebook and the same kind of severe black rectangular purse that my grandmother carried to church. My father had the impression that she had placed two apple pies in the oven,

removed her gingham apron and stuck a pencil stub behind her ear, and then drove to the schoolhouse. She
had metamorphosed from a grandmother to a reporter
without a wasted gesture.

But then, he thought, this is just the sort of reporter
the *Tipton Enterprise* requires. Miz Stoner here is not
going to frighten our local citizenry or irritate them with
uppity manners and citified ways. If she can gain the
confidence of her subjects, they will trust her instinc-
tively.

So, sitting now beside her on the green park bench
beneath the maple tree in front of the schoolhouse, my
father felt a twinge of regret. It might be fun to trade
wisecracks with a mile-a-minute Joan Blondell; but instead of that, he would have to go gently with this easy-
voiced matronly lady whose gray eyes looked watery
and uncertain behind the square rimless bifocals that
kept sliding down her nose.

He gave her the necessary preliminary information—
his name, age, address, professional resume, and so
forth—and then added idly: "I really don't know why
Virgil called you up. There's no good reason for me to
have my name in the newspaper."

She looked at him over her glasses in a way that suggested her myopia perceived him only as a shifting outline of ghostly steam. "How long have you known Virgil
Campbell?" she asked.

"I'm not sure," he replied. "About fifteen years, I'd
guess."

"As a personal friend? Or are you a business associate?"

"Oh no," he said, "I'm not in business. I'm a schoolteacher. You can't call that a business. You can just
barely call it a profession."

She gave him a long mild stare. "But you do admit to being a personal friend?"

"I've always been proud to say so." But he was disconcerted to notice that she wrote his answer down.

"You know, of course, that Mr. Campbell is reputed to be a highly successful bootlegger?"

"I've heard rumors, yes," he admitted. "But I've never seen any evidence of it. And since I'm not a revenue agent, I haven't found it my duty to inquire." He watched her scribble. "Why are you writing this down?" he said. "I don't want to be quoted about gossip in the newspapers. Anyhow, I thought you were a friend of his."

"Oh, Virgil and I go back a long way together," she said and gave him such a warm maternal smile that he felt for a moment that she had put her arm around his shoulder.

"I'm glad to hear that," he said.

"Now, do you think it's proper for a public schoolteacher to be so personally involved with a prominent local bootlegger?"

"Just a dadblame minute now," he said. He began to form the impression that his end of the green park bench was sinking into the ground while Dora Stoner's was rising like the lighter end of a seesaw. "You said Virgil Campbell was a bootlegger. I didn't say that. I never even mentioned the word. I'm proud to be his friend the way a lot of people are. Good citizens, I mean." He breathed a bit huffily, thinking, This interview is going so badly that I'm lining myself up on the side of "good solid citizens." I ought to be ashamed.

She nodded, as if in firm and willing agreement. "Yes," she said. "And do you think it's fair to say that

Mr. Campbell fancies himself something of a king-maker?"

"How do you mean?"

"Is it fair to say he believes that he has some large personal influence in local and state politics, that he is able to secure political appointments and deliver votes?"

"That's the way he talks sometimes. I'm not sure how much of what he says is true. Is it?"

"Is it what?"

"Is what he says true?"

She shook her head. "Oh, I wouldn't know," she said sweetly. "I don't think I've heard him make explicit claims. I'm not sure he'd discuss politics with a woman."

My father laughed. "Virgil will talk politics with a sweaty hound dog asleep in the road," he said.

"Maybe it's just me then," she said and leaned once more to write in her notebook, sliding her glasses back up the bridge of her nose with her index finger.

"Look here now," my father said. "I don't want to be quoted about Virgil in the newspaper. This is all personal stuff, and I've got no interest in politics. I'm just an ordinary fellow trying to get along in the world. If I've got any political opinions, they're private. I don't want folks reading about them at the breakfast table."

"And do you?"

"Do I what?"

"Have any political opinions?"

"Yes," he said and was stricken to see her scribble another note. "What are you writing down about my politics?" he cried.

"Not much," she said, "but I have heard that you're a royalist."

"A royalist? Where did you get that idea?"

"Didn't you once describe George Washington as a

traitor to King George III and declare that he ought to be hung?"

"Yes. I once employed that strategy in a Civics class to underline the fact that there are two sides to every conflict. I was trying to get the kids to understand how the British might have felt about our War of Independence."

"Isn't it possible that you might have been misunderstood?"

"That's always possible. But my effort was to try to be clear. I can't be responsible for every misinterpretation. Look here, I wish you wouldn't put all this in the newspaper."

She was scratching on her paper at a blinding speed. "Oh, this is not going into the newspaper," she said.

"What are you doing then?"

"This is all background information," she said. "The kind of thing our local Democratic Party is interested in. I'm sort of a reporter for them, too. I do find it interesting that you want to keep your political beliefs private. You're not ashamed of them, are you?"

"No. I'm a Democrat too, if that makes any difference."

"As a matter of fact, it does," she said. "I'd like to hear your ideas about Governor Forrest's new plans for broadening the curriculum of public high school education."

"Why? Who'd ever be interested in what I think about that?"

"You might be surprised. After all, you're an experienced science teacher, you must have some thoughts about the new emphasis on science and mathematics."

"No."

"No thoughts whatsoever?"

"I mean, no, I'm not a teacher."

"No?"

"Not anymore. I just quit."

"Just now? You quit teaching just now?"

"About ten minutes ago."

"Why?"

"Well, it's kind of complicated. . . ."

But he did his level best to try to shape his story into a logical sequence. Sometimes it was comprehensible to him, while at other times it seemed as slambang silly as a comic strip. It made sense to fish the little girl out of the creek, but why had he fooled around half the afternoon with that goat? The more he tried to explain them, the lamer his motives appeared, and he saw that he was portraying himself as a creature of mad impulse, someone whose helpless destination was the interior of a spacious butterfly net. And once his story was told, it was told; there was no way to untell it, no way to make himself look good. He ended with a mumbled brief statement: "And that's why I did it."

"Did what?" asked Dora Stoner.

"Quit."

"Quit teaching?"

"Yes."

"For good?"

"I don't think they'd be interested in rehiring me."

"But even if you're not a teacher, you'll still have ideas about public education."

"I suppose so," he said. "I've got opinions the world hasn't even heard rumors of."

"I'm glad to know it. You'll need fresh ideas if you take this new job as head of the Governor's Commission."

"Excuse me?"

She slid her glasses up her nose and left off writing in

her notebook. She turned to face Joe Robert. "I'll bet that Mr. Campbell didn't tell you about what's happened. You're going to be asked to head up the Governor's Special Commission on Education. Did you know that?"

"Is this the truth?"

"Yes."

"Why would they want somebody like me, teaching high school up here in the thickets and hollers? Why don't they get some university specialist?"

"They need somebody who teaches high school and knows the problems firsthand. They don't want some overpaid expert that real high school teachers might resent. And they want somebody who's in favor of the sciences. Just fits you to a T, the way I see it."

"Well, I am flabbergasted."

"You have a right to be," said Dora Stoner.

"How did they ever hear of me here in this old tumbledown schoolhouse? All that's holding the place together is chalk dust."

"Because of the governor's grandniece."

"Who is she?"

"That's the little girl you rescued from the river this morning."

"Well, I'll be—hornswoggled."

"Prettily said."

"I didn't know that's who that little girl was!"

"Not much way you could," she said and once more poised her pencil stub above her notebook page. "So how does it feel to save the governor's grandniece from drowning in the river? Our readers will be interested."

"It wasn't a river," he said. "It was merely Trivet Creek, which is not very big."

"In the newspaper, it will rise in status. It sounds a lot

better to say that your brave exploit took place in a river.
A creek is too piddling for the head of a Governor's Special Commission.''

"I have not done any brave exploits," my father said,
almost in anger. "I already told that to Virgil."

"Well, maybe whatever it was you did perform will
have to rise in status, too," she said. "We want to make
you look good."

My father leaned over and placed his elbows on his
knees and rested his chin in the palms of his hands. He
sat looking into the lambent green grass and hearing bird
song rise throbbing from a distant line of oaks and then
from the field downhill, the mutter and shout of the
baseball game. The light now in midafternoon was ting-
ing yellow, and he felt it as the color of summer coming
on and then the season after summer and the other seasons balanced perilous in time like an avalanche.

Finally, he spoke again. "I want to get it straight in my
mind. The little girl that I pulled out of Trivet Creek and
not any river whatsoever this morning is doing okay.
She did not die of exposure or pneumonia. Her name is
Appleton, according to what Virgil said, and she is the
grandniece of Governor Forrest, according to what you
say. The Democratic Party believes that because I fished
this child out of the water, I have become a world-beater
expert on public secondary school education. So they
will persuade the governor to appoint me head of a Special Commission and give me a Cadillac car to ride
around in on official business."

"Well, I don't know about the Cadillac," she said.
"That might be a little extravagant."

"There will be a Cadillac car attached to it somewhere," he replied mournfully. "Because I told some
possum hunters early this morning that there would be.

All day long I have been trying to tell a lie and I haven't had even a whiff of success. It would be difficult for me to explain to you how nearly impossible it is to tell a lie."

"I know a lot of people who find it possible."

"Like me," my father said. "Used to, I could tell a dozen lies before breakfast and not even break a sweat. But here lately I seem to have lost my touch. Do you think I'm growing old?"

She gave him another of her long mild stares. "No," she said. "I'm not certain, in fact, that you're quite grown up."

"I assure you that I am."

"That's what I'm going to write in the newspaper," she said. "Whether it's true or not." She stood up and closed her notebook.

He looked up at her in wonderment. "Is the interview over?"

"Is there something else you'd like to confess?"

"Good Lord, no. I've said way too much. I can see that. But what are you going to write about this Special Commission deal? Even if you're right and they offer it to me, I'm not sure I'd accept."

"That's not for publication," she said. "First you get to be a hero, then they make you into a bureaucrat."

"I don't want to be either one. I'd like to be an ace scientist or an entrepreneur of major ideas or something in that line. That's what I really want."

"Then I'm sure you'll be successful."

He stood up and awkwardly offered his hand, which she took with a characteristically maternal expression. "Well, I thank you for talking to me," he said. "I wish I was better at interviews."

"It was very refreshing," she said. "You probably wouldn't understand how much I enjoyed it."

After the interview, he sat for a while on the bench, trying to collect his thoughts. But he had no thoughts to collect, only impressions and garbled memories of this long day, which still had a long way to go. In a while, the sounds of the baseball game down the hill attracted his attention and he wandered over the grassy slope, breathing the smells of dust and grass and yellow sunlight.

Janie Forbes was sitting in the third row of the splintery bleacher seats behind home plate and watching the game so intently that she did not even notice my father as he swung casually over the first seats and sat beside her.

"Who's ahead?" he asked.

She gave a breathy little cluck. "Oh, Mr. Kirkman," she said, shading the phrase with as tragic a tone as any mourning dove hidden in a misty autumn dawn.

"Good afternoon. I thought your boyfriend was nothing but a dumb fullback. Now I find out they've got him playing left field, too. That's where they put the real dullards, isn't it? I wonder if he's proud to be dumb and ugly in two sports at the same time."

"He's hitting .388," she said. "And he plays basketball, too."

"If he told you that he is hitting .388 in basketball, then he is merely a gay deceiver and not to be trusted. I credited you with better sense, Janie."

"He used to be a gay deceiver," she said, "but I have
made an honest man out of him."

"How do you mean?"

"Oh, I can't tell you that." She turned to face him full
on and gave him what must have been the wickedest,
most-knowing wink in her arsenal. My father judged it
to be highly effective; it certainly deflected his attention
from his other concerns.

"What can't you tell me?"

"Don't be tricky now," she said. "What I can't tell you
is the thing I can't tell you."

It came to him then, as simple and plain as a single
cloud in a high blue sky. "Never mind," he said. "I
know what it is. You're pregnant, aren't you?"

"Yep." She flashed him a proud lazy smile, then
squirmed away to see a close play at second base. "He's
out!" she called.

"Ah well," my father said. "I do hope that dumb
lunkhead is going to do the right thing and marry up
with you."

She looked at him in pure blank astonishment, then
broke into a strange twittery giggle that descended into a
full contralto open laugh. "Mr. Kirkman," she said, "Larry
and I have been married almost two whole years now."

"You have?"

"I married him the first weekend after I met him. After I
interviewed him one Thursday afternoon for the *Bear
Tracks*, we made a date to get married on Saturday night in
Spartanburg, South Carolina. It was love at first sight."

"That's mighty romantic," my father said. "A secret
marriage."

"Well, it's supposed to be secret," she said. "But I think
you're about the only one around here who doesn't know,
Mr. Kirkman. It's just like you not to know."

He pondered that insightful comment for a moment, then grinned. "But I do know one thing, Janie. It's a revelation that just came to me. I know who you are— you're Ann Onnie Mouse."

A quick endearing flush clouded her face like milk poured into coffee. "How'd you know that?" she said. "Not that I am. Not that I'm confessing."

"It just came to me," he said. "It all fits together."

Last year, when he had been trying to found the governing of this school upon strict experimental scientific principles, there had arisen something of a scandal concerning the school newspaper, *Bear Tracks*. Tucked away at the bottom of a mimeographed column had appeared a quatrain that some of the teachers had considered to be spicy and others to be scandalous. My father had thought it innocuous, but he had been sharply curious about the authorship. It was signed "Ann Onnie Mouse."

> *Twinkle, twinkle, little star,*
> *We went riding in his car.*
> *What we did I ain't admittin'*
> *But what I'm knittin' ain't for Britain.*

Three of the older lady teachers went in a group to demand that he find out who had perpetrated such obscenity, and he had solemnly promised them that he would investigate. But it was transparently clear to them as he spoke that he wasn't going to do a blessed thing about it, wasn't going to stir an inch. That was only one more thing that rankled them about him.

"I do hope that you are going to keep this wild guesswork to yourself," Janie said. "I would hate to think that you're going to go around spreading filthy rumors about me."

"Not me. With a dumb ugly husband like Larry Carruthers, you've got all the trouble you can handle."

"Oh, he's no trouble once you know the magic words."

"What are they?" he asked, knowing full well that he shouldn't ask.

She gave him an innocent glance, as arch as any kindergartener. "Why, *soup's on*, of course," she said. "What else did you ever think?"

They fell silent again to watch the game, but my father's head was so filled with new thoughts and strange information that he couldn't really follow the play. He asked again, "Who's ahead?"

"We are," Janie said. "We're beating them six to three in the seventh inning. We're going to win this one, Mr. Kirkman."

"I'm glad," he said. "I'm glad to hear it." And indeed he felt such a rush of gratification at hearing this lonesome fact that the blood gathered warm about his heart and his face flushed and two tears squeezed from his eyes and ran on his cheek till he furtively brushed them off with his fingertips. Here he sat with Janie to watch her all-too-youthful husband play ball. They had to keep their marriage secret because married girls weren't allowed to attend high school. That was another silly rule, one more that needed changing. Here were other students sitting in the makeshift stands and shouting to the players, and students sitting on car hoods in the bordering parking lot, others stretched out on their stomachs in the grass in the yellowing sunlight, propped on their elbows to watch the fielders and the runners. It came to him again now, as forcibly as it ever had, that this job of

teaching school was the best job in the world, that no
other profession could offer such opportunity or such
satisfaction. No other vocation could offer such true and
invisible honor. "But I do have to admit, though, Janie,
that there's one thing I'm kind of regretful about."

She nodded without looking away from the game. "I
know there is, Mr. Kirkman." Her voice was quiet but
never sad.

"I really had high hopes that you would be going to
college. Woman's College, maybe, down in Greensboro,
or the University of Tennessee. I could have written letters to help get you in."

"I know how you felt about it," she said.

"Not many girls have much chance to go to college
from around here. I was thinking that you would be
kind of an example for them. Because you really do have
the capability, you know."

She looked at him now and nodded shyly. "I'd
planned to go. I was going to make a scientist of myself
just so that you would be proud of me. You remember:
Eva Curie."

He smiled, recollecting a particular class discussion.
"Eva Curie," he murmured.

"But then I fell in love with Larry and went all sloppy
inside and here we are married. I reckon that I'm about
to wind up a barefoot hillbilly woman with a yardful of
younguns and a dishpan full of dirty diapers."

"Is that the way it's going to be then?"

"I'm afraid so."

"You don't seem much downcast at the prospect. I
might even say you're looking forward to it."

"I'll bet it would be fun to be a woman scientist of
great fame and distinction in the science books," she
said. "I'll bet that one day I'll be telling my own kids

what I should have done and what they ought to do. But it turned out that I fell in love and it satisfies my heart to be in love and have all of Larry's children that I can stand to look at. The way it's going to turn out is that one of them will be Eva Curie."

"How do you know?"

"Because I had the chance and I'll always know I had the chance. So that means that any one of them that cares to try will have a double chance. I'll be careful to see to it."

"How about Larry? What'll he think about it?"

"He'll think the right things," she said. "I'll be careful to see to that, too."

"You've got it all figured out then."

"Yes."

"What if it doesn't work?"

"Then I'll have to figure out something else. Are you going to come to my wedding?"

"What wedding? You're already married."

"That was secret. We're going to have a public wedding four weeks from now. A June wedding. We'd be proud to have you come, you and Mrs. Kirkman."

"We'll be proud to be coming. What are you going to name your baby?"

"I thought maybe Eva if it's a girl," she said. "But Larry might have a different idea."

"If it's a boy, I've got a crackerjack name all picked out for you."

"No you haven't."

"Yes I have, too."

"Mr. Kirkman, I am not going to name any child of mine Izambard Kingdom Carruthers, so you can just forget about it."

His tone indicated his sorrowful disappointment, his

profound aggrievement. "Well, why not, I'd like to know? It has a noble ring about it, seems to me. If I was having any more children—"

"Oh hush," she said. "Here's Larry coming to bat. He's going to hit a home run." She then shouted this happy instruction to her husband.

"He looks too big and clumsy to me," my father said. "He's a sure strikeout."

"Lordy, Mr. Kirkman, you're just *awful* today. Maybe it's a lucky thing for everybody that you quit teaching school. You'd be too cranky to put up with."

"How in the world did you know that? I only quit teaching half an hour ago. I haven't told anybody. Or not anybody that you'd know."

"Everybody knows what you did," she said. "Everybody knew as soon as it happened."

"I don't understand this," he said. "Everybody knows everything but me."

"That's twice right. Everybody knows and you don't understand."

He waved at the ball game. "I understand that good old Larry has taken two called strikes. This is some heavy hitter you've got yourself hitched up with. What did you say his average was?"

She ignored these remarks and called out to Larry to make his relationship with the baseball one of murderous ferocity. But Larry only stepped back from the plate as the ball came low inside. "You don't want to be grousing while he's at bat," she said. "Holler it up a little."

"I don't holler," he said. "It's inelegant. It's ungentlemanly. It is primitive. But I will waggle my fingers."

Came then the obliging belt-high pitch over the plate

and Larry stepped into it as into a revolving door and swung his bat as if he was giving a towering long-leaf pine tree the felling stroke and the ball came off his bat in a spatter of sunburst and with a noise like a pumpkin dropped from a church steeple and soared into the cloudless blue sky like a rocket going up on Flag Day and flashed out of sight behind the outfield and landed in a place so distant that not even the most intrepid of geographers has yet located it.

He drove in three runs with that one, but before Larry took his regal home-run trot, he turned around and winked at Janie Forbes Carruthers and blew a kiss.

She turned again to look at my father and to gaze deep into his eyes. "So there now, Mr. Kirkman, tell me what you think."

"Not bad, not bad at all," my father admitted. "I wish he wouldn't blow kisses at me, though. That's bound to start up some ugly rumors. But maybe he'd like to make the acquaintance of a goat I happen to know."

"What do you care?" Janie asked. "You're not a schoolteacher anymore. You don't have to worry about what people think."

"That's right, I'm not." He felt then as if he had been condemned to outer darkness, exiled from the affections of rational humanity. He was no longer a schoolteacher; he didn't count for much.

The score held in favor of Tipton; the game ended and Janie went off to find Larry. The players and coaches, the spectators and umpires departed. Still my father sat behind home plate, looking spellbound into the empty diamond. The clay base paths shone bright orange in this light that had become tawny and autumnal. There was a motion of easy breeze and he fancied for a moment that he felt a breath of chill in it, a hint of winter coming on, but the impression was too silly and he shrugged it off. Yet he kept sitting there, looking before him, looking at nothing.

He was fatigued. It had been a long time since he had slept, he had not managed to eat lunch, and this long rueful day had thrown at him a relentless barrage of low blows and rabbit punches. He had kept ducking and shuffling in his characteristic way, but he had absorbed what he considered a fair amount of punishment. That sort of ceaseless drubbing takes it out of you, he thought. A man needs some time between rounds; he needs a chance to step back and reflect and gather his strength. The unexamined life wasn't worth a plugged nickel; Socrates was right.

No he wasn't. He had met all he ever cared to of Socrates. "Socrates," he muttered, "can kiss my rusty dirt-farming ass." Then he glanced around to see if anyone might have overheard him, but there was no one. The field was as empty as a graveyard on a Monday morning.

We don't need skeptics here, he thought, we need enlightenment. Down with Socrates; long live Prometheus.

The name of the fire-bringer: He needed no more than this, and the customary swagger began to return to my father's thoughts. If everything everywhere looked dark now, that situation was inevitable. It would take this century a long time to recover from the enormous jagged bloody wounds it had given itself. But it was beginning to recover, wasn't it? Look at Janie Forbes Carruthers: There's a smart girl, and she's putting her money on the next generation.

He rose and trudged wearily away from the ball field

up the hill into the schoolyard, keeping his eyes fixed on
the ground, on his feet coming down and lifting like the
pistons of an unfaltering machine. He merely glanced at
the schoolhouse with its darkened windows and angled
corners cutting sharp shadows in the light; he merely
glanced at it as he passed by and went to the parking lot,
but the image of the building in this light would remain
in his head for a long time.

He got into the pickup truck and cranked it up and
rolled away. This was the usual hour when his day ran
backwards. Each day as he drove away from school, the
frets and worries of the place lifted away from him. The
farther he drove from school, the less he was a schoolteacher; the closer he got to home, to our farm, the more
he was a farmer.

So now he began to think ahead, as the amber-glow-
ing landscape rivered by him, the tops of the trees golden
in the cool light, the sun laying its broad swathes of late
light against the hillsides and the farther blue mountains.
At home, there were chores to do: feeding the pigs and
horses and milking the cows and pouring up the milk
and washing the big cans and the buckets. We would be
there too, his family awaiting his return, and he had better be thinking of some sort of mischief to devil us with if
he didn't want us to become complacent. He wondered
what we had been up to all day long, what sort of ad-
ventures had fallen to our lot, and then he came to the
conclusion, was possessed by the solemn conviction that
nothing had happened to us. How could it? Since we
had stayed in bed all day long, we had slept through the
whole thing. He had a vision of us tucked up in the
blankets. He had a picture of me tumbled in my narrow
bed with my books of Vergil, never rising from midnight
till the next dusk, lying awash in a dream of my father

as Aeneas as he descended into the underworld to meet
the dead and rose into the light to talk with the gods
and battled the backward barbarian forces so that civilization might find a foothold in a scrannel and un-
promising soil.

Seeing these pictures in his mind, he drove unnoticing
along the shadowy river road and through the quietened
town of Tipton until he came to where the road crossed
Trivet Creek, with Virgil Campbell's grocery store on the
other side of the bridge. He really ought to stop in to talk
with the old fellow, but the hour was late. He wanted to
get home. And he didn't know what he could say to his
friend; he couldn't decide whether he was grateful to
him or vexed.

So he turned right and poured on the gas, bouncing
dangerously on the rough gravel road as he sped toward
our house. There on the left was the cold drowning millrace he'd pulled the little girl from early this morning,
such a long time ago it seemed. And up on the hill on his
right, glowing with the last bright rays of the sunset, was
John McGlashin's old barn with the little new hay shed
down below it that the dour farmer had built just last
month. . . .

Whoa.

Whoa!

He put on the brakes as quickly as he could without
smashing up and stopped and leaped out of the cab and
clambered up the roadcut to the top of the bank. He was
sure he had seen fire there, flames licking at the fence
where the fence post joined the new hay shed. At the top
of the bank he plunged through the barbwire fence, tearing his overalls and skin unmercifully. But when he
stood up again and got a good look, there was something
odd about the fire. It took a few nervous moments for

him to discover that it was not destructive flames he was
seeing.

It was two red foxes, a vixen and her mate. They were
frisking together in the sunset light, which made them
glow yellow and orange; it was like a powdered fire, the
tips of the separate hairs glowing gold and silver and red.
They jumped and trotted round and round one another,
sniffing and shaking their heads, their amber eyes shining like gems of rosin. My father watched as they curled
and uncurled, leaping over and under one another. Their
brushes flared red in the sunset, their tails were fire-
brands. They flowed into and out of one another like
streams of water aflame.

He kept on watching till the sunset was gone and gray
dusk shadowed all this hill. Then he blinked three times
and when he opened his eyes at last, the foxes were
gone. He turned and squeezed carefully through the
fence and went down the bank to his truck.

He started the motor.

He sat staring through the windshield, his foot holding
the clutch in.

That was the sign he had been looking for, wasn't it?
In the first place, it wiped out his whole debt to the
Crazy Creek Wildlife Appreciation Committee. He had
seen his first fox of the year two times; that was worth
the whole thousand dollars. But it was more than that. It
was the sign that Jubal Henry had promised to him, and
he needed to understand what it meant.

He pulled away from the ditch and drove toward
home, going very slowly now, no more than fifteen
miles an hour. He decided that he knew what it meant:
the foxes that were flames meant that he had done the
right thing, he had made the correct choices. This vision
was an affirmation.

He was finished with teaching and with everything to do with teaching. He wouldn't go back, not for Socrates, not for the governor of North Carolina, not even for Janie Forbes Carruthers. He was through with demonstrating, illustrating, and explaining. He had stopped talking and now he was going to deal directly. He was going to lay his own personal hands on the world.

Watch out, William Cavendish and Luther Burbank and William Buckland. Move over, Izambard Kingdom Brunel.

Here comes Joe Robert Kirkman, and who can say what will happen, what tongue can tell?

DARWIN

Dr. Charles Darwin was physically a smaller man than my father had imagined him to be and when the two impassive policemen brought him out of the basement boiler room and up the steps into the back schoolyard, his unsteady pace suggested the effects of his famous but mysterious infirmity. The scaffold was waiting there in the cindered enclosure and the members of the school board were watching from the top landing of the fire escape. Irene Macclesfield, Susie Underwood, Handy Conrad, Ben Meaders, Jack Coble, Cole Smathers—all were present and they looked down upon the scene with stern anticipation.

On the scaffold, my father waited, and it seemed to take hours for the naturalist to mount the steps and advance across the platform. After a brief glance at my father and a serene nod, he kept his gaze fixed on the arm of the gibbet. He regarded it mildly, as if it was an object of scientific curiosity. He seemed without fear or apprehension. Even when one of the policemen lowered the rope from the gibbet arm and the other pulled the hangnoose round his neck, Dr. Darwin did not show the least discomposure.

My father, however, was in a state. Right here and now behind Tipton High School, they were going to hang one of the greatest minds the human race had produced unless, performing at the top of his powers of reasonable persuasion, he could change the minds of the school board members, convincing them to alter their mortal sentence. It seemed an impossible task. But he stepped forward to the edge of the scaffold, looked up to the top of the fire escape where the board members stood waiting to respond, and began his brilliant defense:

"On all sides," he said, "I hear the cry: We are men and women, not a mere better sort of ape, just a bit bigger in brain than your chimpanzees and gorillas. The power of knowledge, the conscience of good and evil, the empathic tenderness of human affections, raise us out of fellowship with the brutes, however closely they may seem to approximate us.

"We are told by some who pretend to religious authority in these matters that the belief in the unity of origin of man and brutes involves the degradation of mankind. But is this really so? Could not a sensible child confute this conclusion? Is it indeed true that the Poet, or the Philosopher, or the Artist whose genius is the glory of his age, is degraded from his high estate by the historical certainty that he is the descendant of some naked savage whose intelligence was just sufficient to make him more cunning than the fox and more

dangerous than the tiger? Or is he bound to howl and grovel on all fours because of the unquestionable fact that he was once an egg that no ordinary power of discrimination could distinguish from that of a dog? Or is the philanthropist or the saint to give up his endeavors to lead a noble life because the simplest study of man's nature reveals at bottom all the selfish passions and fierce appetites of the quadruped? Is mother love vile because a hen shows it, or fidelity base because dogs possess it?

"The common sense of the mass of mankind will answer these questions without a moment's hesitation. Healthy humanity, finding itself hard pressed to escape from real sin and degradation, will leave the brooding over speculative squabbling to the cynics and the professionally self-righteous who, disagreeing in everything else, unite in blindness to the nobility of the visible world and in insensibility to the grandeur of the place man occupies."

My father produced a capacious red bandanna from the back pocket of his overalls. He now noticed for the first time that he was wearing the motley soiled outfit he'd worn all day at school and that plaster dust dribbled out of his hair onto his shoulders when he blotted his forehead. Even so, he thought he was doing pretty well. He couldn't quite make out the faces of the school board members aloft yonder, but he thought that he detected a softening of attitude among them, a warming of their sympathies. The stolid policeman by the fateful lever that could spring the trap beneath Dr. Darwin stood at attention.

Joe Robert felt certain that he was making strong headway and continued speaking with fresh confidence.

"But thoughtful persons, once escaped from the influences of prejudice, will find in the lowly stock from which man sprang the best evidence of the splendor of his capacities, and will discern in his long progress through the past a

solid reasonable ground of faith in his attainment of a brighter future.

"These observers will remember that in comparing civilized man with the animal world, one is like the Alpine traveler who sees the mountains soaring into the sky and can hardly discern where the deep shadowed crags and roseate peaks end and where the clouds of heaven begin. Surely the awestruck voyager may be excused if at first he refuses to believe the geologist who tells him that these glorious masses are only the hardened mud of primeval seas, or the cooled slag of subterranean furnaces merely raised by inward forces to that place of seemingly inaccessible glory.

"But the geologist is right; and due reflection on his teachings, instead of diminishing our reverence and our wonder, adds all the force of intellectual sublimity to the aesthetic intuition of the beholder."

I've got them now, my father thought, I've got them eating out of my hand. I'll go down in history as the orator who saved Charles Darwin from an ignominious lynching in Tipton, North Carolina.

He sneaked a peek at the policeman who stood by the lever and, though his facial expression remained unreadable, his posture seemed more relaxed now and his hand was held carefully away from the long wooden lever with its black velvet-wrapped handle.

One final effort is all we need, he thought. I'm going to win this one at last.

"And after passion and prejudice have died away," he continued, "the same result will attend the teachings of the naturalist respecting that great Everest of the living world—Man."

But as he spoke this sentence, he felt a premonitory quiver start at the base of his spine and work its way swiftly toward the top of his skull.

Oh no, he thought. Oh no.

"Our reverence—our . . . reverence, I say, will—will not—cannot—be . . . lessened— . . ."

He scrubbed the cold sweat from his neck with the red bandanna. He had laid it on too thick and now his mind and spirit and body revolted. He could not continue in this defense. He did not believe a syllable of what he had said, that was the trouble. The foreknowledge of what he was going to say next was a burning embarrassment, but he could not stop himself.

"And yet man delights not me," he said, "no, nor woman, neither. The more favorably I speak of our species, the more its history gives me the lie. The briefest glance at our record discovers us to be steeped in blood and reveling in it. We have enjoyed naming compassion weakness and have murdered with full public assent the wisest and most humane of our teachers; we have imagined a monstrous God who regrets that he must torture certain numbers of us during the whole compass of eternity; we have embraced an idea of justice that glories in bloody retribution. We choose war as the final arbiter among political philosophies, and wage it against our civilian populations, our children and our parents. The best of our ideals we have made into excuses to kill our own kind and the other animals along with ourselves."

He had lost all control now; he was no longer the author of his own words, but only the vessel of a Truth that had long been waiting to make him its spokesman.

"The fact is that Dr. Darwin was mistaken. We did not begin as blobs of simple slime and work up to higher states. We began as innocent germs and added to our original nature cunning, deceit, self-loathing, treachery, betrayal, murder, and blasphemy. We began lowly and have fallen from even that humble estate. Dr. Darwin has searched for the truth. It is the nature of the human animal to subject

its earnest seekers and most passionate thinkers to humiliation, degradation, imprisonment, and execution. If you now condemn this great man to death, you shall be guilty of nothing more than your own most ordinary humanity.''

He had wanted to say everything differently, something cheerful and original. But it was too late.

The weary-faced policeman pulled the lever and the trap fell open. Dr. Charles Darwin hovered in the air for a few ridiculous seconds, gave a small embarrassed farewell gesture with one hand, and said in a tiny mousy voice: ''Bye-bye.'' Then he plummeted from sight like a dropped cannonball.

My father giggled in his sleep and chortled, shifted in the bed and nudged my mother with his elbow. Did she understand? Did she get the joke?

But she did not respond. My mother, too, was dreaming, busy with her own concerns, pursuing her own exotic life.